D1246184

FIRE TRAP

A T.J. PETERSON MYSTERY

BOB KROLL

COPYRIGHT © BOB KROLL, 2019

PUBLISHED BY ECW PRESS
665 GERRARD STREET EAST
TORONTO, ONTARIO M4M 1Y2
416-694-3348 / INFO@ECWPRESS.COM

ALL RIGHTS RESERVED. NO PART OF THIS PUBLICATION MAY BE REPRODUCED, STORED IN A RETRIEVAL SYSTEM, OR TRANSMITTED IN ANY FORM BY ANY PROCESS — ELECTRONIC, MECHANICAL, PHOTOCOPYING, RECORDING, OR OTHERWISE — WITHOUT THE PRIOR WRITTEN PERMISSION OF THE COPYRIGHT OWNERS AND ECW PRESS. THE SCANNING, UPLOADING, AND DISTRIBUTION OF THIS BOOK VIA THE INTERNET OR VIA ANY OTHER MEANS WITHOUT THE PERMISSION OF THE PUBLISHER IS ILLEGAL AND PUNISHABLE BY LAW. PLEASE PURCHASE ONLY AUTHORIZED ELECTRONIC EDITIONS, AND DO NOT PARTICIPATE IN OR ENCOURAGE ELECTRONIC PIRACY OF COPYRIGHTED MATERIALS. YOUR SUPPORT OF THE AUTHOR'S RIGHTS IS APPRECIATED.

COVER DESIGN: CYANOTYPE
AUTHOR PHOTO: MARY REARDON

THIS IS A WORK OF FICTION. NAMES, CHARACTERS, PLACES, AND INCIDENTS EITHER ARE THE PRODUCT OF THE AUTHOR'S IMAGINATION OR ARE USED FICTITIOUSLY, AND ANY RESEMBLANCE TO ACTUAL PERSONS, LIVING OR DEAD, BUSINESS ESTABLISHMENTS, EVENTS, OR LOCALES IS ENTIRELY COINCIDENTAL.

LIBRARY AND ARCHIVES CANADA CATALOGUING IN PUBLICATION

TITLE: FIRE TRAP / BOB KROLL.

NAMES: KROLL, BOB, 1947– AUTHOR.

DESCRIPTION: SERIES STATEMENT: A T.J. PETERSON MYSTERY ; 3

IDENTIFIERS: CANADIANA (PRINT) 20190109106 CANADIANA (EBOOK) 20190109114

ISBN 9781770414891 (SOFTCOVER)
ISBN 9781773053929 (PDF)
ISBN 9781773053912 (EPUB)

CLASSIFICATION: LCC PS8621.R644 F57 2019
DDC C813/.6–DC23

THE PUBLICATION OF **FIRE TRAP** HAS BEEN GENEROUSLY SUPPORTED BY THE CANADA COUNCIL FOR THE ARTS WHICH LAST YEAR INVESTED $153 MILLION TO BRING THE ARTS TO CANADIANS THROUGHOUT THE COUNTRY AND IS FUNDED IN PART BY THE GOVERNMENT OF CANADA. *NOUS REMERCIONS LE CONSEIL DES ARTS DU CANADA DE SON SOUTIEN. L'AN DERNIER, LE CONSEIL A INVESTI 153 MILLIONS DE DOLLARS POUR METTRE DE L'ART DANS LA VIE DES CANADIENNES ET DES CANADIENS DE TOUT LE PAYS. CE LIVRE EST FINANCÉ EN PARTIE PAR LE GOUVERNEMENT DU CANADA.* WE ACKNOWLEDGE THE SUPPORT OF THE ONTARIO ARTS COUNCIL (OAC), AN AGENCY OF THE GOVERNMENT OF ONTARIO, WHICH LAST YEAR FUNDED 1,737 INDIVIDUAL ARTISTS AND 1,095 ORGANIZATIONS IN 223 COMMUNITIES ACROSS ONTARIO FOR A TOTAL OF $52.1 MILLION. WE ALSO ACKNOWLEDGE THE CONTRIBUTION OF THE GOVERNMENT OF ONTARIO THROUGH THE ONTARIO BOOK PUBLISHING TAX CREDIT, AND THROUGH ONTARIO CREATES FOR THE MARKETING OF THIS BOOK.

ONTARIO ARTS COUNCIL
CONSEIL DES ARTS DE L'ONTARIO
an Ontario government agency
un organisme du gouvernement de l'Ontario

Canada Council
for the Arts

Conseil des Arts
du Canada

Canada

PRINTED AND BOUND IN CANADA

PRINTING: NORECOB   5   4   3   2   1

MIX
Paper from
responsible sources
FSC
www.fsc.org   FSC® C103560

CHAPTER
ONE

He followed. Insecure. Feeling jinxed among the dried cornstalks. Feeling lost in a corn maze in blazing sunlight. A dead end and a wrong turn. Another, and then another, spiralling Peterson and Patty Creaser back to where they had started. She laughed and plunged back into the maze.

Another wrong turn, another dead end, and he trampled into the cornstalks to bushwhack his own path.

"Stop," Patty hollered.

He turned to her, and as he did so, the phone in his brown field coat pocket rang. It rang a second time, and she looked for him to answer it. He shook his head to say he was not going to. He knew who it was, who it always was, and he did not want to hear her silence or see another photo of the hellhole his daughter was living in, not another unmade bed pushed into a corner of a filthy narrow room with brown stained walls, not another side table with a cupped piece of aluminum foil, syringe, and rubber tubing on top.

Patty stiffened and turned away from him.

The phone rang again, and he saw the cords in the back of her neck tighten. She flipped her brown hair then ran her fingers through it, fixing it to hide the surgical scar along the right side of her face.

The phone rang a fourth time, and Peterson looked directly at the sun as though it could burn all the images of all his daughter's filthy rooms from his mind, as though it could purify his daughter's life, purify his own.

His phone stopped ringing, and he saw Patty had already walked away from him and farther into the maze.

• • •

They drove the back roads past lush vineyards with dark purple grapes, past apple orchards heavy with ripening fruit, and past variegated green fields of cabbage, kale, and broccoli. Peterson's attention went between the curving road and the rearview, keeping an eye on a dark blue Ford Explorer that had been following them since the corn maze, probably before that. He pulled over and stopped beside a roadside stand so Patty could buy a pumpkin. The Explorer slowed as it passed. All Peterson noticed about the driver was that he had long hair. The passenger was another man, shaved head, and he was hanging out the window and holding up his phone like a camera. As the SUV drove off, Peterson saw it had British Columbia plates, with the licence number beginning with EDP.

"Your daughter is keeping contact," Patty was saying as she climbed from the car. "She doesn't have to, but she is."

He watched the Explorer drive out of sight. Then he got out too.

The fruit and vegetable stand was a five-by-twelve-foot shed with wooden bins of pumpkins on either side — unattended. There was a hammer and a cream-coloured jug on one of the windowsills, and cobwebs in the corners of the glass. A handwritten sign on a nearby tree informed customers that sales were on the honour system. Large pumpkins were five dollars; everything else was three. The various-sized pumpkins were all mixed together in two bins. It was up to customers to decide how large a pumpkin was and how much they were to pay.

"It's her way of asking for help," Patty insisted.

His ex-cop brain had gone into overdrive about the Explorer. He remembered a similar one parked across from the Homestead Restaurant, where they had lunched.

"You don't think she's asking for help?" she said.

He poked around in one of the bins. "I don't know what Katy is doing." He pulled a large pumpkin from the bin and held it up for Patty to see. Patty shook her head, and he replaced the pumpkin in the bin.

Patty selected a similar-sized pumpkin. "You don't want to talk about it." She put the pumpkin back.

He dug deeper into the bin.

"That's the problem," she said. "You don't want to talk about anything that matters, not about your daughter, not about yourself. You won't even talk about us. You cut it short when it needs talking about."

He dug deeper into the bin and withdrew a larger pumpkin. He held it up. "How about this one?"

Patty grabbed the pumpkin and smashed it at his feet, then walked to the car and got in.

He considered the smashed pumpkin. He looked at her. He looked down the road to where the Ford Explorer had driven out of sight. He reached for his wallet, pulled a ten, and dropped it into an old cigar box with a note taped on top: "Make your own change."

He got into the car. "This is not about my daughter, is it?"

Patty would not look at him.

They drove back to the city in silence. He parked outside a high-rise and walked her to the door and into the lobby. She offered to make him coffee, but he shook his head. "Why drag it out?"

Patty agreed.

● ● ●

He drove the streets of downtown Halifax for a while, and then walked them, the way he had walked them for days and weeks after his daughter had run away, searching the faces of the passersby. He saw three young women exit the ferry terminal. Black stretch pants and coloured shirts reaching to mid-thigh. Two had shoulder-length brown hair. The third wore hers cut short. She had a pouty face and a way of waving her right hand when she spoke, which reminded him of his daughter.

He followed the three women into Stayner's Restaurant, stood near a coat rack, and watched the hostess seat them at a table in the centre of the dining room. The young woman who reminded him of his daughter sat facing him. He wished his daughter would call him just then, so he could hear her silence as he stared at this young woman.

The young woman looked up, and he averted his eyes. After a long moment, he looked back to see her laughing at something one of the other two must have said, laughing happily the way he had seldom seen his daughter laugh.

"Table for one?" the hostess asked.

He looked at her and shook his head.

CHAPTER
TWO

Dave Cotter, a jumbo behind the bar, was closing up, washing beer glasses, drying them, and sliding them into an overhead rack. He owned the place, a blue-collar and no-collar pub in the north end, and worked it 24-7, a retired cop who lived upstairs, alone.

"A peace bond won't do your sister any good," he said to Janice Doyle, who was stacking chairs on tables.

Her ankles were swollen and her legs tired. She was a lifer to waitressing. She wore the job like a crown of thorns, her mouth twisted into a perpetual frown that broke into a half-baked smile only for her favourite customers.

"And of course you know better than her lawyer?" she fired back.

"You don't think I ran into these characters on the job?" he said, rinsing a glass in a sink behind the bar. "Your sister gets a peace bond, and he's loading up a Remington. And right now, you're bunking at her place to keep her company."

Peterson stood in the doorway. Darts to one side, VLTs to the other. In a far corner there was a ceiling-mounted TV for sports nuts.

Doyle saw Peterson, dropped him a half dip, and cocked him a pistol point that went along with her big grin. More than once Peterson had done her a good turn, and her payback to him was treating him like a standout compared to anyone else that walked through the front door. Besides that, she downright liked him.

Cotter was still talking. "You know how many of these guys, their paperwork crossed my desk. They backhand their old lady, then go all whiney after she hits the floor. They're all alike. I'm telling you a peace bond won't stop him. He's off the wall, Janice. Your sister could end up in a box. And you could be right there in another."

"Who you talking about?" Peterson asked as he walked to the bar and sat down.

"Janice's sister has a new boyfriend," Cotter said, pulling a black coffee from an urn behind the bar and setting it in front of Peterson. He looked at Janice. "Walter Barlow. You want to tell him?"

"My sister Ellen caught him doing some things, and kicked him out," she said.

"He got rough with her," Cotter added, polishing a glass and racking it. "A sex nut. The guy said he was an English professor, for Christ's sake. I thought all of them were celibate. He brought home another girl and wanted a threesome. Take pictures. Make a movie. The sister blew up, walked out. She came home an hour later, and this Barlow

11

and the other woman were naked on the couch. What the hell's it coming to? When I was married, you never brought them home."

"And you wonder why your wives all left," Janice said. She went behind the bar for her brown shoulder bag and pink sweater. She looked at Peterson. "My sister's no angel, but she didn't deserve getting beat up."

Cotter leaned toward Peterson. "It's all the sex people see on the Internet, magazines in the grocery stores. Instructions on how many ways to turn him on."

Doyle looked at the ceiling and shook her head. She set her bag on the bar and pulled on her sweater.

"Tell him what else the boyfriend's into," Cotter said.

"You're the one with the dirty mouth," she said.

"What dirty mouth? I'm talking to Peterson, for God's sake. He was on the job, working the street half his life. He seen things I don't even know about." He turned to Peterson. "He forced Ellen to watch this sicko shit on his laptop. Whips and chains. He wanted her to join a club he's in."

"She wouldn't join," Doyle insisted.

"He left behind the laptop with all his dirty pictures," Cotter said.

"He called a few times, asked if she gave it to anyone," Doyle said. "She has it, but she's afraid he'll come to get it."

"What do you think?" Peterson asked.

"I think he won't come around with me staying there."

"I said the two of them should stay here," Cotter piped. "I got a spare room, double bed. No, better yet, the two of you should bunk at Peterson's." He looked at Peterson. "What's with the eyes? You don't go home, not to sleep. Half the time you're driving the streets all night."

"You can't live with your sister forever," Peterson said to her.

"When she gets the peace bond, I'll go home," she said.

"Sure, that'll hold him back," Cotter scoffed.

"Are you worried?" Peterson asked.

"A little," Doyle said, and pointed at Cotter. "And he makes it worse."

Cotter made a face and dried a glass. "Anybody who teaches English all day is bound to have something loose upstairs."

"I'm leaving," Doyle called. She waved and left the place.

Cotter turned to Peterson. "Another nutcase. The world is full of them. And that reminds me, Ziggy was looking for you."

"Did he say why?" Peterson sipped the coffee.

"Between the lines. He comes in spouting that religious crap about Hell and damnation. Then he does that cross-eyed thing and says you're good at solving people's problems. And I said to him, yeah, but sometimes not everyone involved comes out in one piece."

Peterson looked at him. "Was that meant to be a compliment?"

"It was meant to be what it is," Cotter said. "You're out there almost every night. It's like you're trying to be a cop again."

Peterson looked at his hands, clawlike around the coffee mug.

"I'm not criticizing," Cotter said, back to washing and rinsing. "I'm just worried about Ziggy saying you now got a problem of your own. What was he talking about? I don't want you going to pieces again, so that nothing, not even those head-shrink sessions can stick you back together. For Christ's sake, you're a man with a past, Peterson, and when it gets loose, it tears you apart."

Peterson eased his grip on the mug. He lifted his head and looked at Cotter. "Thanks for the vote of confidence."

Cotter stopped washing and rinsing. "Maybe I know too much."

Peterson shifted his gaze and saw himself in the mirror behind the bar. He closed his eyes for a moment, then opened them.

"Ziggy still living in his tin can?" he asked.

Cotter folded the washcloth and set it on a shelf beneath the bar. "I don't know how he can live like that. I'll tell you something else. I don't know how you can live the way you do."

Peterson pulled his three-by-six black notebook and a pen from his jacket pocket and wrote the make and model of the SUV that had been following him, along with the three letters of the licence plate. He tore the page from the notebook and slid it across the bar.

Cotter read it and said, "Is this a problem I should worry about?"

Peterson shook his head. "I'm just curious, and these days my curiosity is using up favours downtown." He again looked at himself in the mirror.

Cotter folded the paper and set it beside the old-fashioned cash register behind the bar. He faced Peterson and leaned in close.

"The trouble with curiosity," he said, "is that it's always trying to live up to its reputation."

CHAPTER
THREE

Peterson parked along a paved road overlooking the Fairview Container Terminal and grabbed a Maglite from a duffle in the back seat. A dirt path ran beneath a highway exit ramp, through a jungle of knotweed, nettles, spiny burdocks, and high bushes. It skirted a disembowelled building and ran alongside piles of rubble and broken furniture and appliances. Then it opened to a small clearing that overlooked the harbour. He shut the Maglite and listened to the tortured squeal of metal on metal from the container terminal. From across the harbour came the sound of a railway switcher shunting cars in a nearby freight yard.

At the far end of the clearing was an abandoned ten-foot shipping container that was badly damaged on both ends. A brown canvas tarp hung from where the double doors had been sheared off.

He hammered on the side of the rusted steel container, and Ziggy Glover threw back the canvas. He held a Coleman lantern above his head. In his other hand was a .22 Colt automatic.

"You expecting someone else?" Peterson asked the parking lot preacher.

"I'm always expecting someone else. Sometimes I'm expecting the Incomprehensible One." Ziggy raised the .22 and the lantern above his shaggy head. "The established truth is immutable. You have to find it."

He swung the lantern and .22 to show the way into a cramped space decked out with a multi-coloured braided rug that had the centre burned out, and a wall that was plastered with mind-messing crayon drawings. He set the lantern on a twelve-inch-wide cable spool, and settled his black-robed body into an overstuffed blue armchair with its guts leaking out. On the floor beside the chair was a red bong. Ziggy pointed for Peterson to sit on a milk crate, then said, "Woe to you because you dwell in darkness and in death."

"From an ex-con, scripture sounds like sacrilege," Peterson said, lowering himself to the milk crate, knees up around his ears.

Ziggy flinched, a look that was small and cold. "One mistake, and I can't live it down."

"Two counts of embezzlement," Peterson corrected. He shifted uncomfortably on the crate.

Ziggy reached behind to a brick-and-board bookcase. His blousy sleeve rode up his arm, showing off a colour tattoo of a serpent swallowing its tail. He held up a thick book.

"I'm preaching truth," Ziggy said. "Words like poetry, and I light them up with fire from the Old Testament. No meaning, but it sounds good, and that's what people want. They want to feel the words, and I lay it on thick. Hallelujah this. Amen that. Cut through the noise with the hand of God touching their hearts. I got over fifty the other night. I passed the hat and got a big score from drunks and head whackers, and some of those Pentecostals who think I'm speaking in tongues. This book has me preaching like I'm snorting, blowing, or sucking six chemicals at once."

Peterson took the book from Ziggy, read the spine — The Nag Hammadi Library — and opened it just anywhere. *The Gospel of Seth*. He read a sentence and threw Ziggy Glover a sceptical look.

"They think I'm a prophet," Ziggy said. "I got it down so tight it comes off like conversation." He threw back his head and raised his arms. "The anguish and the terror fills you for all the wickedness you have done."

Ziggy flashed a mischievous smile. "They think I'm Moses, and they're lining up to tell me their sins. I got a pipeline to the street like I never had."

"That means you're still selling information."

"A man's got to eat, only these days nobody with a badge is listening."

Peterson turned to another page in the book, *The Gospel of Thomas*. He leaned into the low-angled light, which deepened the lines in his fifty-two-year-old face. He scowled at what he read.

"The pipeline goes nowhere," Ziggy was saying. "Deaf ears. You hear what I'm saying? Drug squad, Vice, they're all looking for headlines."

"Always did."

"After the easy score."

"Uh huh." Peterson had heard it all before — snitches complaining that command and investigating officers weren't listening.

"And your former partner? Not the same anymore," Ziggy said, wagging an index finger.

"Eyes on the brass ring," Peterson explained.

"Picking low hanging fruit is what Danny Little's doing," Ziggy said. "You and him together broke rules to get it done right. Now he's puppy-dogging to get ahead."

Peterson leaned forward on the milk crate. "Cotter said you wanted to see me."

Ziggy shook his head and gestured for him to be cool. He returned the book to the bookshelf, then took a hit off the bong, held the smoke, then blew it out. "Do you remember Andy Benson?"

Peterson faked a laugh. "How could I forget?"

"Yeah, he got what he deserved. But in the end, we all get what we deserve. But there is a light that is hidden in the silence. Only Benson is shining it on you."

"Tell him to take a number."

Ziggy threw back his head and belly laughed.

"Badass," he said. "You descended down into the midst of the underworld and broke free from the chains of the demons." He lifted the bong. "I heard Benson has someone to play with, a maniac."

"Got a name?"

"No name. But I heard they like the same toys."

"Another porn boy chalking up film credits," Peterson said.

"No play-acting no more. Reality TV. Benson now goes dirty and deep. Internet. That's where the money is. Rolling up the film tax credit cleared the field. Equipment went for fire sale prices. First come, first served, and Benson had a semi parked at the back door. Big time studio to go with it. "

"Is this something you're selling?"

"Like I said, no one's buying. I just thought you should know. Grudge match."

"Is that why I'm here?"

Ziggy blinked behind the magnifiers. Removed them and rubbed his eyes. He put his glasses back on and again reached behind to the bookcase. This time he removed an iPhone in a brown leather case.

"A woman came to hear me preach," Ziggy said. "She knew what I do on the side. She showed me the phone and held out her hand. She wanted a hundred bucks for an unlocked phone. That's what makes it a score, but I don't know if it's been used and abused, and if the cops already got a tap on it. So I jewed her down to forty dollars, enough to buy herself something sweet."

Ziggy took another hit off the bong.

Peterson waited patiently.

"So I scroll the contacts," Ziggy said through a cough of smoke. "Guess whose name is on the list?"

Peterson frowned.

"I checked her phone log too," Ziggy said. "Does Britney Comer ring a bell?"

Peterson nodded. "It's been a long time."

"Not that long. Her last outgoing call was three days ago, to you."

Peterson thought about all the calls he had been ignoring over the past few weeks. Hers would have been one of them. Then he wondered why Britney Comer had called him.

Ziggy must have enjoyed seeing Peterson's reaction because now he leaned forward and whispered, "I checked her incoming calls. You never called her, not after she called you, and not before, not as far back as the log went. But someone did."

He settled into the overstuffed chair. Big smile.

Peterson tried not to look too interested, but the longer Ziggy held back from saying, the more Peterson itched to know.

"It came with a caller ID," Ziggy finally said. "Andrew Benson." He stretched out his arms in a gesture of benediction. "Blessed is he who takes the Lord's stand against the evildoers."

Peterson looked around Ziggy's eight-by-ten-foot corrugated container. It was crummy, dingy, and rust and shadows were climbing the walls. "How much?" he asked.

Ziggy made a scoop move with his hips and said, "She reports that phone lost or stolen, her server cuts off the number. Call goes through, that phone is money." He passed Peterson the phone.

Peterson dialled his cell on Comer's phone. His phone vibrated.

Ziggy flashed a big grin. "The list price is a hundred bucks. But just for you, I'll make today discount day. Call it eighty."

"You already told me what I need to know. Her message is on my phone."

Ziggy settled deeper into the overstuffed chair, his face now in shadow. "And he was seized by the hope that does not exist."

Peterson got up, pulled out his wallet, and stuffed four twenties through a slot in the milk crate. "Donation," he said, and threw aside the canvas cover on the door.

Ziggy flashed a holier-than-thou smile. "He lies in wait like a beast in a thicket. Let us pray."

Peterson turned back into the lantern light. The half tones on one side of his face and the liquid darkness behind him emphasized his tired and abandoned look.

CHAPTER
FOUR

He got into his car and set Britney Comer's phone on the dash. Then he pulled his own and tapped to retrieve his voice messages. There were four of them. One was three days old. One had come in yesterday. The other two he had received that afternoon as he and Patty were puzzling their way through the corn maze.

He played one of today's messages and heard his daughter breathing. Nothing said. Just her short breaths, and a camera shot of a long dirty hallway with an exit sign at the far end.

He played the second of today's messages. His daughter again. More breathing. The same for yesterday's message, only this one came with a different camera shot — a fly squashed on a windowpane. Then he played the message that was three days old. It was from Britney Comer.

She said who she was. Her voice sounded nervous, and he sensed that she had been reading the words she was saying. She apologized for not having called him before this, explaining that she had kept in touch with his daughter since Katy had left home and gone to Vancouver. She said she had good news about Katy and asked him to call her.

● ● ●

Tracking down Britney Comer's address took one call to a friend on the force, a desk sergeant working the night shift. Another used-up favour. The sergeant ran Comer's name through the Motor Vehicle database. She lived in a five-year-old apartment building on Kaye Street, amidst a trendy commercial area of cafés, restaurants, and boutiques. When Peterson checked the lobby directory, he saw that she shared the apartment with Jeremy Mains. It was Mains who answered the intercom.

"Hello?"

"My name is Peterson. I'm Katy Peterson's father. Britney left me a message that she had good news about my daughter. Is Britney there?"

There was a long silence, then Mains said, "No, she's not here."

Peterson noted the crack in Mains's voice.

"What's wrong?"

There was another long silence, then Mains said, "She hasn't been home in two days."

"Buzz me in," Peterson insisted. "I'm an ex-cop."

Maybe it was the word *cop* that triggered Mains's immediate response, or maybe the authority in Peterson's voice.

The lobby door buzzed and clicked, and Peterson entered. He took the elevator to the third floor, and walked a hallway with beige-painted walls and white-painted doorframes and baseboards. Mains stood outside the open door to 302, shifting from foot to foot. Early thirties, body of a heavy-duty jogger, thick brown hair tousled in that messy look.

Peterson held out his hand and Mains shook it. Mains had a glazed look like someone who had not slept in days. Peterson gestured for them to enter the apartment, and Mains led the way through a short hallway to the living room.

Chrome-framed Ansel Adams repros of Yosemite National Park on the wall. Heavy Mission Style furniture that spoke of money and a man's taste, a sure sign to Peterson that Britney Comer had done the moving in. Mains sat in the oak-frame recliner with beige and brown upholstery. Peterson pegged it as *his* chair. He took the matching love seat and leaned forward over the glass-topped oak coffee table.

"Tell me what happened," he said.

Mains stared at him for a moment, then said, "That's what the police asked when they were here. They made it sound like it was me." His voice rose. "Nothing happened. I went to work. She was working on a story. I came home. She didn't. Nothing since. Not a call."

Comer's phone message to him was not a card Peterson wanted to play just yet. "And that was two days ago?" He tried for consoling, but too many years as a cop had drained most of the comfort from his voice.

Mains looked like he had a dazed brain. Finally he said, "Two days."

"What did the police say?"

"Nothing. They wanted to know if we argued, if I got violent, for God's sake."

"Did you?"

"No!"

Peterson saw the strained look on the young man's face, and heard the anxiety in his voice. He knew why the police had questioned Mains the way they had. A husband or boyfriend was often the reason a woman ran away from home.

The father of a teenage girl was also on that list of people women ran away from, he thought. That dredged up the memory of the female cop sitting across from him in his own living room. Blue flowered couch and stuffed armchairs. Matching drapes. Family photos on the wall behind the mahogany credenza. Crystal decanter and stemware on top. His wife's favourite room. Not his. Never was.

The cop's face had gone stern when she had asked if he and Katy had argued that night.

That was three years ago. No, it was longer than that. It was nearly six years since his wife had died in a car accident on the Shore Road, crushed to death by an overturned cement truck. Six years, and his daughter still blamed him for her mother's death. As he saw it, she was using her spazzed-out life to get even.

Yes, he had answered the female cop, they had argued that night. What he didn't say was that he had locked her in the basement to prevent her from going out to get high. Not thinking she had a phone. Screaming at him through the door that she called 911. Letting her out, and her running from the house and shouting "Fuck You!" from the sidewalk.

25

He closed his eyes and saw himself ringing up every teen hangout and hellhole that he knew about. Every god-damn crack house and condemned building in the city.

He opened his eyes to see Mains sitting in the oak frame recliner.

"You said she was covering a story," Peterson said.

Mains looked up from his hands folded on his lap.

"More than one," he said. "She's freelancing and has to keep as many on the go as she can handle."

Present tense, Peterson thought. Present tense is good.

"Like what?"

"A story on prostitutes," Mains said. "She's also working on a piece about food banks for CTV, and then something political. She's upset about that one."

"Upset?"

"She won't talk about it." Mains suddenly looked at Peterson as though seeing him for the first time. "Who did you say you were?"

"Peterson. Katy Peterson is my daughter. Britney left me a message that she had good news about my daughter. That's why I'm here."

The confusion left the young man's face.

"Britney talked about her," he said. "Old friends."

"High school friends," Peterson said.

"She was in trouble of some kind. Something Brit felt bad about."

Peterson let it go. "Did Britney say anything about what the good news could be?"

"No. But I know your daughter called the other day. It wasn't her phone, not from caller ID. The call caught Brit by surprise. I couldn't tell if she was happy about it or not."

"Did she say what they talked about?"

Mains shook his head, then rolled his hands, palms up. He looked at them. He looked at Peterson. "I don't know what to do," he appealed. His face went to mush. He started to weep, then caught himself. "The police said to give it a few more days, but I don't think they're doing anything."

"Yes they are. Believe me, they want to find her as much as you do."

"But they won't say she's a missing person."

"Right now she just didn't come home. In most cases the person shows up within seventy-two hours. Sometimes wives, girlfriends just need a break. Then they come home flashing up an I'm sorry smile." The last bit he sugar-coated, knowing damn well that most women return because they have nowhere else to go.

Mains nodded, unconvinced. "They don't tell me what they're doing."

Because you're a suspect, Peterson thought, but would not say. Instead, he offered, "They don't want you worrying more than you already are."

"How can I worry more than I am?"

Peterson let the question hang for a moment then changed gears. "How long have you been together?"

Mains blinked as though not understanding the question. Finally he said, "Almost two years."

"When did she move in?"

"Last month. This place is a lot bigger than hers. The spare bedroom is her office. She didn't have one where she was living."

"And what do you do?"

"Me?"

"What do you work at?"

"Investment counsellor for Scotia McLeod."

"Keeps you busy."

Mains nodded.

"Were you home when she left the apartment?"

Mains shook his head. "I went to work early. She was in her office."

"That was Saturday," Peterson said.

"I work a lot of Saturdays. Overtime is a must."

"Was she fine with that?"

"She works more than me, day and night," he said, and Peterson had the impression Mains was not too thrilled about that. "Freelance is a pain. She's out there digging up stories that don't sell."

"When she left the apartment, do you have any idea where she was going?" Peterson asked.

"She was meeting someone she wasn't too excited about."

"Why's that?"

Tears filled the young man's eyes. "No idea," he said.

"Do you know who she was meeting?"

"I wasn't really listening. I was running late." He gave a sad smile. "We slept in. Not many mornings when we do."

Peterson nodded, tried to remember when he and his wife were first married. Days off. Only getting out of bed to eat. Pregnancy put an end to that. A daughter. Careers. How soon it falls apart. "Can I look at her office?" he asked.

"The office?"

"There might be something in there that could help."

Mains did not say yes, no, or maybe. He just sat in the chair, bent forward, chin in his hands. Confused.

Peterson had conducted more than enough interrogations to know when a suspect was lying like truth, or telling it just the way it was. He judged Mains was the latter, and that the young man was truly worried. Peterson got up and went to the spare room that Comer used as an office. Mains got up and followed him.

A cluttered journalist's office. Bookcase that was chockablock, and more books stacked on the floor. Dark brown desk with the veneer peeled on one corner, piled high with newspapers and magazines. An Epson printer. Half a dozen yellow pencils and an equal number of Bic pens. No desktop computer. No laptop. *Probably takes the laptop with her*, he thought. There was a pad of legal-sized paper with nothing written on it. Under the pad was a multi-page environmental assessment report for a resort and marina along the eastern shore. He turned to the last page and read that the assessment board had recommended the construction, and that the environment minister had approved it.

On the right side of the desk was a reporter's notebook. Only half a dozen pages had been written on. These contained what he took to be dates and times, along with initials, for meetings or interviews. There was a page of statistics about food bank shortages along with annual food donations for the past five years.

On the next-to-last page he read: *Z has a contact that could break things open. Worried. Not worried. Anxious.* He felt Mains at his shoulder and turned to him. "She has a note about someone named Z. Any idea who she means?"

"She's the woman Brit is working with on the prostitution story," Mains explained. "Zola something."

Peterson knew Stephanie Zola — late twenties, former prostitute — who ran a counselling service to help girls get off the street.

Halfway down the page were the initials *TC* along with the number *3*. Peterson assumed the *3* meant the time of day for a meeting. He thought maybe *TC* were her father's initials — Tim Comer. There was no date, and no indication of where. An arrow ran from the initials up the page to the word *email*.

At the bottom of the page, written on an angle across three lines, as though scribbled in a hurry, were the words *Horseshoe* and *creepy boyfriend*.

Peterson pulled a pen and a small black notebook from his jacket pocket and jotted down a few notes. He injected a smile into his voice. "I hope you're not the creepy boyfriend?"

Mains covered his mouth and shook his head.

Peterson studied him. Real emotion. Real tears. "How's her mother taking it?"

That caught Mains by surprise, and the look that folded over the young man's face told Peterson that Mains had not told Comer's mother. "They don't get along very well," Mains said.

Peterson did not doubt that for an instant, having known the mother since they were teens, growing up together on the eastern shore. Raylene O'Connell, married to Tim Comer; O'Connell the director of the Provincial Arts Council and board member of the Tourism Industry Association of Nova Scotia, Tim Comer a backroom political consultant, Peterson considered telling the mother himself, then decided against it, preferring, for the short term at least, to leave things as they were.

"I don't think she's taking a break from me," Mains said, as though just now catching up with the conversation.

Peterson studied him.

"It's been good," Mains added. He looked hard at Peterson. "She would've said something."

CHAPTER
FIVE

He drove the route he took most nights, not breaking routine. Checking the rearview for anyone following him.

He drove past a boarded up St. Pat's Elementary, where a group of teens were taking turns in the shadows. He knew what they were doing. Rolling on rubbers and growing up fast to lives played out in what they watched. Small screens. Big screens. Squeezing their asses tight to the online sleaze that was poking out their eyes.

He slowed as he went by. They were too young to know who the hell he was. A cop with notches to his name, ghosts playing grab-ass inside his head.

He swung up the entrance ramp to the bridge at the narrow end of the harbour and sailed through the toll with a bridge pass. Gunned it along an interchange, took the third exit, and slowed to a crawl along a four-lane, which at this hour was still firing on four barrels with its foot to the floor. Across his windscreen flared coloured lights from fast food joints serving pill poppers and arm stabbers too stoned to keep loading up. There were tat studios and sleaze shops, a peeler bar with a backroom for screw and runs, and a Mickey D's where junior highs were juking to a rapper rhythm and calling it homework.

High beams flashed and horns blasted for him to step on it. His eyes flipped between road and rearview. Aggravated drivers passed. Finger salutes. He was in no hurry, and he was sure as hell not worried about someone blowing up with road rage.

Across the overpass, the four-lane cooled down through a residential stretch. He made a few random turns then slowed into a windy coastal road that led to a crescent beach. He parked and looked out on the distant city lights undulating on the tide in the harbour. Waves over the cobbles were clicking in retreat. Power plant stacks were belching white clouds with black linings of crusty ash.

He sat in the dark for more than an hour, playing shell games with faces he stored in the back of his mind. Dead faces of young women he had failed. Molly Gornish and Mickey Mac, Debbie Wilson and Tanya Colpitts. And then he saw the wide-eyed face of the drug dealer in the container terminal, shaking up a terrified smile until Peterson fired point blank and blew it off.

He reached for his phone and played the voice message again and then again. He remembered Britney Comer coming in and out of his house with his daughter. Britney always singing. Playing herself like Hannah Montana. Elementary School. Junior High. Katy disgruntled with him, with her mother. Dressing in rags from the Sally Ann. Precious smile when she shared one. A crooked tooth he should have had fixed. And deep brown eyes that saw through him.

His daughter's high school years had been lost to him. She and Britney locking themselves in Katy's room. Posing nude. Boyfriend offering tabs and dots for screen shots of tits and ass. The girls smoking up and popping whatever pill Andy Benson had given them, whatever would keep their feet from touching down. Katy coming home to sleep, and often not even doing that. Sixteen and living on the street and what went with it. Playing it like it was a game.

A game, for Christ's sake!

He gripped the steering wheel hard at the thought of it. Still hearing his wife blaming him, and him shrugging her off with a bottle of Johnnie Walker.

Britney had straightened herself out, back to school, journalism degree. Katy had remained strung out in a spiral that brought her lower and lower. And he had been no better. Hitting rock bottom after his wife died and his daughter ran away to her hellish life on the West Coast.

Suddenly he saw his daughter the way he had seen so many with caked-over eyes and pincushion arms. He got out of the car and stood there shaking. Then he got hold of himself and got back in the car and drove into the city, to a west end neighbourhood of post-war pre-fabs. He parked and opened the glove box to a pint of Johnnie Walker. Unbroken seal. A comfort knowing it was there, security if and when he needed it. He closed the glove box, slid his seat back, and, with his arms folded on his chest, shut his eyes.

CHAPTER
SIX

His car was parked across the street from where Janice's sister lived in a small yellow bungalow, in a neighbourhood of similar-sized pre-fab houses. He woke in the back seat and lay there looking through the rear window at a black sky faint with stars, remembering another time he'd woken up in the back seat of a car and how frightened he had been at the bullet hole in the roof, at the smell of cordite in the car, and at the loaded .38 on his chest with the safety off.

The memory of that waking still frightened him. He rubbed a hand over his stubbled face and through his greying hair. The car clock read 5:45 a.m. There was a duffle bag he had used as a pillow — his camping kit, he called it — and from the bag he pulled a toothbrush and a bottle of Listerine. He ran the dry toothbrush over his teeth, took a mouthful of Listerine, returned the bottle to the bag, then got out and spit.

He stood outside the car waiting and watching the house. When a light went on toward the back of the house, he waited a few minutes more, then went to a door off the driveway, where the kitchen was.

Ellen Doyle answered the door holding a cup of coffee and wearing jeans and a blue cotton blouse.

"I'm Peterson."

She nodded and a length of brown hair fell over her right eye. "Janice said you would come."

"I was parked across the street half the night."

"She said you would do that too."

"She knows me too well."

She held up her coffee mug. "You want one?"

He nodded and followed her into a small kitchen that hearkened back to the 1980s. Knotty pine cupboards. Green chipped Formica counter top. She poured him a mug of coffee. They sat in ladder-back chairs, at a maple table edged with cigarette burns. She lit one and dragged deeply.

"I'm trying," she said, "but I got to have one with morning coffee. You smoke?"

"I have other vices."

"I'll bet you do," she said, and smiled flirtatiously.

"You have some of your own," he said.

She tapped an ash into a mocha-coloured ashtray. "Did Janice tell you that?"

"In so many words."

"Do you think that's an excuse for him hitting me?"

"I'm just framing a picture," he said.

She dragged on the cigarette. Blew it out. "He was in a

36

club, group sex, some of it looked rough. He showed me videos thinking it would interest me. It didn't. Then he brought a woman here and said if I tried it, I might like it. I told him what I thought. That's when he hit me."

"What about the laptop?"

"It was in a shoulder bag he carries."

"He probably wants it back," Peterson said.

"I know."

"Did he threaten you?"

"That's why I'm getting a peace bond."

"It's a piece of paper, Ellen. It works on some people, not all, and I can't keep sleeping outside your house."

"You can always come in."

"Not likely," he said.

She faked a frown.

"Give me the shoulder bag, and I'll make sure he doesn't come back. Write down his address."

She paused a moment. "I didn't get it."

Peterson frowned. "At least you got his name?"

Doyle looked away. "That wasn't fair." She looked back. "He said his name was Walter Barlow. He said he teaches English Literature at St. Mary's."

"Did you believe that?" he asked.

She shrugged. "I wanted to." She went for her phone on the table and searched online for Barlow's address. She read it to him, and he wrote it in his notebook.

"Now what?" she asked.

"You go back to living the life you were living."

She retrieved the shoulder bag from another room and passed it to him.

"Scumbags come in all shapes and sizes," he said.

"Knowing how to read them should be part of every woman's education. They take advantage, Ellen."

He tossed the shoulder bag into the back seat of the Chevy and got in. He still had the feeling of being followed, still with the blue Ford Explorer in his mind, the driver with long hair and the male passenger with the shaved head.

He swung in and out of side streets, across the MacDonald Bridge over the harbour, then back again, through parking lots, up the on-ramp to the 102, then down the first exit ramp, then up again, then down again, finally parking at a Shoppers Drug Mart, reaching for Walter Barlow's shoulder bag in the back seat, walking three blocks, cutting through a backyard, and entering his own house through the back door.

He only used the blue two-storey to shower and shave, change his clothes, check his emails — no idea why since his daughter was the only one he received them from. He seldom slept there, and when he did, it was in the brown leather recliner in the den. Sometimes he curled up on the matching love seat. Mostly he drove around the streets all night, sometimes crashing at Cotter's place above The Office, a few times at Patty's apartment. Going home was something he found difficult to do. The house came with memories.

Cotter had understood when Peterson had told him that. He had nodded and replied, "You never know when one of them will slip from a closet and club you from behind."

In the den, Peterson dropped Barlow's shoulder bag on the leather love seat. From his field coat pocket, he pulled his cell phone and set it on a dark oak desk beside an iMac.

He fired up his computer, opened his mail file, and saw that his daughter had not only Skyped him on his cell phone, but also sent him an email. The email contained the photo of a long dark hallway with a red exit sign at the far end. The Skype call and the email were her way of cutting him twice with the same knife. He dragged the photo into a folder on his desktop, which contained most of the photos his daughter had emailed him over the past three and a half years. It was an estranged father's reluctant way of imagining himself into her life.

He closed the iMac and went upstairs to shower, shave, and change into beige chinos and a grey work shirt.

He returned to the den, sat in the recliner, and reached for Walter Barlow's brown leather shoulder bag. Everything about it said new: new leather smell and no wear and tear on the strap or the reinforced corners. There was an eight-by-eleven-inch pad of yellow lined paper in the bag, as well as several different coloured felt markers and a three-by-five-inch black memo pad. The yellow lined pad had not been touched, and only the first page of the memo pad had been written on. It contained web addresses.

The laptop seemed new, unused at least. The software was what came preloaded. There were no files. It seemed Barlow had only used the laptop for accessing the Internet.

Peterson wondered about the new bag and new laptop. He saw Barlow as a man creating a separate life, a fantasy world he could access from wherever and whenever he liked. Web addresses instead of bookmarks. No traces. No back end. A fiction in his made-up world.

He opened the Safari browser and keyed in the web address for the first of three websites listed in the notebook. The home page came with a come-on disguised as a warning, about shocking hot sex on the inside. It promised virgins defiled for the first time. There was a sidebar with soft porn video of young women fondling themselves. He entered the site and navigated through several pages, seeing nothing he hadn't seen twenty years before, during his two-year stint in Vice.

The second site offered some hardcore porn. On the third site the porn revved up to what Vice Squad had always referred to as the "whacko shit." This site exacted a five-dollar entrance fee, charged to a credit card that was already on file, a convenient click and pay system for the horny hard-ons with only their hands to love.

Peterson entered on Barlow's dime. It was what he had expected. Whips and chains, and a lot of men shouting at women and women shouting at men. The dominant women dressed in black leathers. They chained men to walls or strapped them to beds or wooden planks. Dominant men appeared as leather-vested marvels and whipped the young pseudo-virgins in the same way the dominatrix had whipped the men. All of it was the same pornographic mindlessness Peterson had investigated years ago. The same slurry of faked orgasms. The same out-of-work and well-endowed young men; the same used and abused young women with habits they couldn't shake, or runaways scooped off the streets on bullshit promises of bright lights and film star credits. What Peterson knew from his years on the job was that it was the same story for most of them, and it sickened him to think about their young lives winding up in cheap motel rooms, digitally immortalized on camera phones and live-streamed to the Net, their pond scum eyes black lined and glistening; their bodies powdered to hide the crack-induced skin sores and self-inflicted scars.

The last sites in the notebook had web addresses that ended with .onion. When he keyed in the address, his browser drew a blank.

He closed the laptop, returned it and the memo pad to the shoulder bag. Then he pulled out his phone and scrolled his contacts list, highlighted one, and hit dial.

No hello on Gross's part, just an expletive uttered from a mouth that sounded like it was full of cotton. Gross asked if Peterson knew what time it was.

"Early," Peterson said.

"Too early, for Christ's sake," his friend said.

"I need to hear the background sound on a phone message," Peterson said, his voice more a command than a statement.

"And like always, you need to hear it now," Gross grumbled.

"How soon can you be at the studio?"

"I got to shower, eat something. Give me an hour."

CHAPTER
SEVEN

Head Games Studios was in a concrete warehouse in an industrial park that was a labyrinth of criss-crossing streets. Peterson was standing beside his car when Harold Desgrosseilliers, whose name, since childhood, had been shortened to Gross, swung his dark green Acura TLX into the parking lot and pulled up to the front door. He squeezed his short two-hundred-and-ten-pound body from the car, looked at Peterson, and ducked his head of stringy blond hair back into the car. This time he came out with a cardboard tray containing two coffees and a bag of donuts.

"Black, right?" Gross said, handing a coffee to Peterson.

The lobby had enough chrome and stainless steel to look like a commercial kitchen. Twelve-foot high white double doors led into a white, open-concept production studio, with eighteen white desks scattered about, each with an iMac on top. Several virtual reality developers were already deep into their monitors.

Gross led Peterson through the white maze to another set of white-painted doors at the opposite end of the production studio.

"What's with all the white?" asked Peterson.

"Interior designer," Gross said. "White is the in thing. My girlfriend had to redecorate our house into white everything. Walls, woodwork. White cupboards and countertops in the kitchen. White bathrooms upstairs and down. Between home and studio, it's like living my life inside a pharmacy. My controller calls this place a whited sepulchre. That's why I work back here in the sound studio. I'm thirty-eight years old, own and operate a multi-mil Virtual Reality company, yet I'm a dinosaur when it comes to the modern world of interior design. I like warm and cozy."

He opened the white double doors into the sound studio, which was in stark contrast to the white production studio they had come from. It had dimmed incandescent recessed lighting, a cork floor, and beige-painted baffled walls. Gross settled into a dark brown leather swivel chair at a huge digital audio board. Peterson took a matching chair beside him.

Peterson knew the file on Harold Desgrosseilliers. His father had been a small-time music producer of local artists. Gross had cut his teeth at the audio board helping his old man mix band tracks. He later excelled at producing music videos, won a few regional music awards, and used that as a springboard into producing television commercials and industrial films. Sammy Sprague, an online game developer, convinced Gross to partner with him in creating virtual reality experiences for clients throughout North America.

Peterson and Gross sipped the coffees, then Gross asked, "So what do you have?"

Peterson held up his cell.

"Like I said on the phone, I received a voice message from a woman. There's something in the background I want to hear."

"Will I get in trouble over this?"

"Not likely. If there's anything, I'll be bringing it to the police."

Peterson scrolled to the voice message and handed Gross the phone.

Gross dumped the message into the audio system. He then ran it through the mixing board and fed the sound to JBL wall speakers. He cued the voice message, slugged his coffee, and hit play.

Peterson closed his eyes and lowered his head as they listened to waves crashing and to Britney Comer's voice telling Peterson she had good news about his daughter. Through the studio speakers, her voice filled the room, and they could hear a slight tremor as she said the words *good news*.

Peterson and Gross sat in silence. Gross was the first to speak. "What's this about?"

Peterson opened his eyes and looked at him. "She's missing."

Gross's voice went soft. "From an ex-homicide detective, that doesn't sound good."

"She's been gone almost four days. That's not good."

Gross got up and walked away from the audio board,

as though being close to the source of the woman's voice might involve him in something he did not want to be involved in.

"Did you hear the other voice?" Peterson asked.

"In the background, behind the waves," Gross said. "The waves were mixed in behind her voice, and I think the other voice was added after that."

"Recorded before the call was made," Peterson added.

"Sounds that way, yeah."

"Can you clean it up?"

Gross breathed deeply and sat back down. He played his hands over the audio board then cued the track. They both closed their eyes and listened.

Comer's voice now sounded muffled. The breakers had been muted, and the other voice, a man's voice, was faint, but clear enough that they both agreed it sounded as though he had said, "Are *you* listening?" Since the call had been made to Peterson, the heavily emphasized "you" must clearly have meant him.

Peterson insisted Gross play it several times just to be sure. Then Gross pulled a couple of thumb drives of the equalized audio and passed them to Peterson.

"You live a screwed-up life," he said. "I would've thought you'd had enough of this crap before you retired."

"I thought so too, but the woman called me."

"And you can't leave it with the police."

"Because I live a screwed-up life."

"For as long as I've known you."

"It gets worse," Peterson said, pulling Walter Barlow's laptop from the shoulder bag and handing it to Gross.

"What now?"

"A guy, an English professor, left this behind after smacking a woman because she wouldn't play sex games with him. Kinky. Multiple partners. He goes online watching this stuff. Keeps track of his websites on a notepad. I had a look but only got so far. There was one website I couldn't access. The address I didn't recognize — dot onion."

"Are you taking this to the police too?" Gross asked.

Peterson shook his head. "Not sure. Not right away."

Gross handed back the laptop.

"Nothing doing on this one, Peterson," he said. "The voice message was on your phone, that's okay. But the laptop isn't yours. I have a four-million-dollar company that could go to seven, maybe ten in a year or two. My clients are worldwide. They're stable and respectable."

He pointed at the laptop.

"That is porn," he said. "An onion website means dark web. And that is someone's laptop. We have privacy laws, and he's probably someone who could sue me into bank-ruptcy if I so much as open it. You already know what this guy's into. And on the dark web he's just going into it deeper and deeper."

"Tell me about the dark web."

"Put the laptop in the bag. I don't even want to look at it."

Peterson returned the laptop to the shoulder bag.

Gross drained his coffee.

Peterson saw the tense look on his face, a risk-taker early in his career, a made-in-Canada entrepreneur, who had now settled into middle age and tightened up.

"I know nothing about style and home furnishings," Gross said, "but with the business I run, that makes no dif-ference. You on the other hand are still trying to work the detective angle in a world you know less and less about. You should accept retirement, Peterson, and let youth do the dirty work."

"Thanks for your advice," Peterson said and got up.

"That's not how I meant it. I'm just saying the world has gone beyond perverted. People are doing some awful shit to one another. They were doing awful shit in your day, I know, but what they're doing today is a hundred times worse."

"Don't bet on it," Peterson challenged. "You have no idea what was on the street then, and what's on the street now. Your mother was a cop, and you have no idea what she ran up against almost every day of her life."

"I know some of it," Gross said. "I know the part that made her take her own life."

Peterson sat down. He regretted the sudden turn the conversation had taken.

"I'm sorry I brought that up," he said.

Gross waved it off. "Maybe that's why I'm being protective," he said. "The child abuse cases got to her. But what she was dealing with was nothing like what's on the web. The underage prostitution, the runaway teens you've been trying to save, the web is full of them. And the dark web, it's a black hole that's just sucking in the worst things you can think of. I had one experience and that was more than enough. A developer I fired, I saw what he was into, creating virtual porn experiences. I had the Mounties in here, a corporal from a special division. I wanted to make sure none of what that developer was doing tarred the reputation of this company. You know what she told me? She said what I saw doesn't even scratch the surface. And you

47

know what else? She said it takes special police training to manoeuvre through Tor or the Onion. That's what the dark web is called. And in this province, there are only two cops trained to do it."

He lifted his cup to drink, saw that it was empty, and crushed it between his hands. He looked at Peterson. "If the cops in the know can't do anything . . . Christ, I don't know what to think. I'm sorry, Peterson, but I want nothing to do with this. That's the first time I had to say that to you."

Peterson stood, and this time Gross stood with him. They walked back through the white double doors and negotiated around the scatter of white desks to the second set of white double doors, which led into the lobby. Gross held out his hand, and Peterson shook it.

Peterson held up the thumb drives with the voice message. "Thanks for this." He pocketed the drives and asked, "Do you remember the name of the Mountie?"

Gross pulled his iPhone from his shirt pocket and scrolled the contacts list. "Corporal Jennifer Collins," he said.

Peterson pulled his notebook and pen from a jacket pocket and wrote down her name and number.

Gross snickered at the pad and paper. "Dinosaur," he said.

Peterson crossed the parking lot to his car. He got in and called a homicide detective named Grace Bernard. They had worked together when he was on the job and a few times after his forced retirement.

"In bed or at your desk?" he asked.

"Is that the best you can do?" she answered. Tired voice.

"I'm short on clever at this time of day. Are you busy?"

"You could say that."

"I have something you should listen to," Peterson enticed.

"You sound like my son with his rap music. What's it about?" she pressed.

"A phone message from a missing person."

"Wrong department," she said.

"Gut feeling. This one might end up on your desk."

"Name?"

"Britney Comer."

"Say again."

"Britney Comer."

There was a momentary pause, then she said, "I'll call you back in five minutes."

It was more like twenty minutes. He was already on the bridge returning to the Halifax side.

"I'm at the parking lot overlooking the cliff at Herring Cove," she said, the banter gone from her voice. "Come right now."

CHAPTER
EIGHT

Detective Grace Bernard led Peterson to the edge of the look-off to see where a cobble footpath broke from a stand of scrub spruce and zig-zagged down the granite cliff. The wind off the water blew stronger here, and the crash of waves on the craggy shoreline was more pronounced.

Peterson looked to where a forensic tech struggled up the footpath carrying a clear plastic bag. Farther down the footpath, Detective Danny Little stood beside a flat-topped rock that rose above the tide, standing in that slumped-shoulder stance he always took when he was working something out.

"How's Danny doing?" Peterson asked.

"Danny's Danny," she said, and faced away from the wind. "He's jumping hoops he doesn't like jumping through. His promotion's almost guaranteed."

He looked at her kindly, knowing half her story. Single mom of a fifteen-year-old. Boyfriend, JTF2 Special Forces killed in Iraq when Canadian troops were not supposed to be there. Ten years on the job, four a detective. Putting up with the male bullshit of fellow cops. Most of that she had told him. The hearsay parts he had ignored.

"And I'll bet Danny's toeing the line so as not to screw anything up," he said.

"He started calling me Detective Bernard." She chuckled. "He said it's more professional. I insisted he keep calling me Bernie like everyone else. He won't."

"Changed man," he said.

"Not for the better."

"What's that supposed to mean?"

"Another time."

"Then why bring it up?"

She chinned toward Peterson's beat-up brown Chevy. "Nice ride?"

"I don't need much more than this."

"Going nowhere, right."

He shrugged.

"Are you still talking with the priest?" she asked.

Peterson nodded. "Along with group sessions with a shrink."

"How are they going?"

"Same direction as everything else." He looked down the footpath to Danny Little. "Twenty-three years we were friends. Then for doing something I can't live with having done, he cuts me off. Explain that to me."

"You crossed a line," Bernie said.

"You don't have enough fingers to count the number of

51

lines Danny and me crossed. I became a head case, and he became a choir boy." He faced her. "What I did that night had to be done."

"You should've called in the cavalry."

He shook his head and looked back at Danny Little standing with his back to the cliff, as though he knew Peterson would be watching him.

"A lot of things I should have done," he said. "And some things I should have done different. The price I paid is living with the hell of it all."

"When was the last time you slept?"

"What's today?"

She smiled. "At least you're still not drinking." The tone in her voice made it a question.

"At least there's that."

"Yeah, but my guess is you're still getting into trouble. Are you and the social worker still an item?"

He shrugged. "Tender hooks." Again he looked down at Danny. "What's this about?"

"A local couple on a morning walk saw what they thought was a body. It turned out to be a woman's clothes carefully laid out to look like one: jeans, yellow sweater, Blundstone boots."

"Prank?"

"The clothes were covered in blood."

"It could be animal blood," Peterson cautioned.

"It could be, but my gut tells me different."

"Woman's intuition," he said.

"Don't you start too," she groaned.

Peterson looked to an outcrop of rock where several uniformed cops were combing the area below it for clues.

"What about the phone message?" Bernie asked.

He turned to her. "It's from a woman whose boyfriend has reported her missing. Britney Comer."

Bernie studied him.

"The clothes the couple found," she said. "Wallet sticking from a sleeve. The driver's licence belongs to Britney Comer."

Peterson turned and saw that Danny Little had started up the path and was not far behind the forensic tech with the clear plastic bag. The two of them squeezed between two huge granite boulders before entering the stand of scrub spruce.

"Tell me about the message," she said.

"Someone must have known that I turn my phone off a lot, avoiding calls from my daughter. And when it's on and I get a call from a number I don't recognize, I don't answer it."

"I don't understand doing that," she said. "She's your daughter."

"Her calls are long silences. I stopped answering months ago. And her Skype calls are always the same, a rundown room she wants to hurt me with. I ignore those too. Eventually they show up in an email. Those I save."

"What about the message?"

"Britney said she had good news about my daughter."

"What good news?"

"She didn't say." Peterson held up a thumb drive he had gotten from Gross. "I heard something in the message that made me curious, so I had a sound studio clean up the audio. You can make out a man's voice saying something in the background."

"Saying what?"

"Saying, 'Are *you* listening?'"

"Are you listening to what?"

"No. The voice emphasized the *you*. It was asking if *I* was listening. The call was to me. He wanted to make sure I was paying close attention."

"I don't understand," she said.

Peterson then explained what Gross had said about the waves and man's voice being added after Comer's message had been recorded. "Probably to make it sound as though she had been near the ocean, like right here."

Bernie thought about it then said, "So this guy knew you don't answer your daughter's calls, and had a recorded message ready to play after the beep."

"So it seems."

"Why?"

He shook his head and stepped closer to the cliff edge and looked out over the water. "Clever way to get me involved," he said. He turned and saw the blue Ford Explorer slowly drive past. The driver had dark, shoulder-length hair. He couldn't make out the passenger.

"What are you looking at?" Bernie asked.

"Someone rubbernecking," he answered as the SUV rounded a curve out of sight.

"Like they don't see enough on the news," she said.

The forensic tech placed the bag of clothes in the side door of the forensic van then got behind the wheel and started the engine. Detective Little walked up to the van and handed the tech something. The van drove off, and Little walked over to Bernie's red Chevy Cruz and waited for them to join him there.

Bernie and Peterson stood on one side of the Civic, Danny stayed on the other. Peterson and Danny stared at

54

each other as Bernie told Little the details about Peterson's phone message from the woman whose bloody clothes had been found on a rock at the water's edge.

"I was wondering if it was the same Britney Comer," Little said. "Now I know." His voice was filled with disdain.

Peterson's eyes had never left Danny's face. "The last I heard, she graduated King's as a journalist and was free-lancing."

"Keeping track?" Little challenged. "Stalking maybe?"

"I heard about her freelancing from a friend."

"You don't have friends," Little taunted.

"We can't all be like you," Peterson said. "Big halo, ducking through doors. Isn't that what you've become?"

"What about what you've become?" Little challenged. "Lone wolf going in with a shotgun down the eastern shore. I don't care what the crime scene looked like."

"According to news reports, they were drug dealers," Peterson defended. "And an old retired cop pulled the trigger."

"Made to look that way."

"You want to start pointing fingers, Dan? I can point fingers too."

Their voices had been climbing, but now Little stepped closer to Peterson and lowered his. "I can live with my past. Can you?"

Peterson's face pained with what he was thinking. Then, in a voice as soft as Danny Little's, he said, "Does that mean all of it, or just the good parts?"

Danny glared at him. "You got a call from a woman, a missing person whose bloody clothes we just bagged. I hope this isn't another one of your mistakes." He walked to his white Malibu parked on the opposite side of the look-off.

Peterson watched him to the car then said to Bernie, "Now you're supposed to tell me my involvement ends here."

"When did you ever take orders?" She smiled.

He smiled back.

"Just play by the rules and keep me informed," she said.

Danny's car peeled from the dirt siding and onto the paved road.

Bernie nodded in that direction. "It was his idea to bring you out here. We could've dealt with the phone call behind a desk, but he wanted to yank your chain. That's what he said. Add another face to your collection. But I'm getting to know him better than that. By getting you involved, especially if you know the victim, you won't let it go. You'll start turning stones we can't turn."

CHAPTER
NINE

He parked near Patty's office and walked to a coffee shop where she often went for her mid-morning break. He grabbed a window seat to wait for her. Feeling apologetic yet unsure about being there, making the first move.

Directly across the street was a derelict red brick building with windows like sightless eyes. The sun was shining on its grubby face.

He looked away, distracted by something that wasn't there. Then he suddenly felt an unexpected flood of emotion at the memory of his mother at a hospital window in a red brick building, waving to him. Waving goodbye. And his father's voice saying, "Because children aren't allowed to go in."

He remembered looking up at that fifth-floor window. He remembered his mother stepping away from it, into a dark emptiness.

He got up and went to the counter and bought a coffee. When he returned to the window seat, he thought better of it and moved to another table with an angled view that did not fully encompass the derelict building. He waited for Patty, his eyes distant with the memory of his mother. Not letting go. Never letting go. A fixture in his mind, like the face of the drug dealer in the container terminal. Never losing its grip.

He pushed the coffee aside, suddenly feeling the point-lessness of being there. He got up and left the coffee shop.

● ● ●

The five of them sat in a tight circle, in a green-painted, sun-filled room, in a closed-down school now used as a community resource building. There was the grey-bearded guy, the woman with butch cut hair, the new guy wearing a Blue Jays cap, Peterson, and the older woman in jeans and a brown chamois shirt that was frayed at the cuffs. She was Dr. Beatrice Heaney, a retired psychiatrist who volunteered to counsel vets and first responders who suffered from PTSD.

"I don't like the dark," the new guy was saying. Late twenties, red-and-blue-checked shirt, his cap pulled low on his forehead, which cast his fearful eyes in shadow. "All the time I got to have the lights on. No surprises. I don't want no surprises."

He looked up from his hands and stared at nothing. The others gave him time to say what he needed to say. He looked back at his hands in order to talk.

"Being a cop was what I wanted since high school,"

he said, his voice cracking. "Now I'm begging to get off the street."

He turned to Peterson, as though appealing to him for support.

Peterson looked at the floor.

"You don't get used to it," the grey bearded guy said. "You never get used to it."

The woman with the butch cut brown hair nodded.

"It comes out of nowhere," grey beard said. "Not so much flashbacks as feelings. Then the feelings trigger what you start seeing up here." He pointed to his head, his grey hair pulled into a ponytail. "A barn outside Sarajevo filled with shoes and coats. Hundreds of them. Some days I can't get out of bed."

"That was war," the new guy said. "This is different."

"The hell it's different," the woman with the butch cut hair said. Hunching into the brown cardigan that was three sizes too long in the sleeves. "Combat is combat. War zone. On the street. It only takes one. And then you go home and everything's different. Nothing's the way it used to be. Not anymore."

The new guy shook his head at her and looked at Peterson, who was still staring at the floor between his feet as though there were something important embedded in the dark grey tile.

The talk went on for a while longer. The others left. Peterson stayed behind. Dr. Heaney removed her cane from the back of her chair and walked over to sit beside him. He was still staring at the floor.

"I take it there is something you did not want the others to hear," she said.

Peterson didn't answer. Shrugged.

Dr. Heaney rolled the cane between her hands.

"Do you want to talk about it?" she asked.

"Are you still recording what we say?"

"Yes. Unless you want me to turn it off."

He tilted back his head and let the sunlight fill his face.

"We were in the container terminal," he said. "I chased him there. I squeezed between a row of containers, came to the end of the row, and turned. We were three feet apart. All I wanted was to get out of there. Go home to my wife and daughter. Then he moved and I pulled the trigger, and I never wanted to go home again."

He grimaced and sat forward. Stared at his hands for a while. Then he got up and left.

When he reached his car, he turned on his phone and saw that he had a message from Raylene O'Connell. He thought about what a loan shark named Jackie Bates once told him, that old friends are the worst kind. They always come back to haunt you.

CHAPTER
TEN

He had to call the house from the front gate of a modest estate called Storm View, and wait for Raylene O'Connell to buzz him in. Then he drove a windy gravel path through a leafy tunnel of red maples. The underwood on either side was a tangle of wild rose bushes and hemlock, a discouragement to those who did not want to use the gate.

"This is not a house for someone who throws a lot of stones," Peterson said to Raylene, who stood at the front door with her arms folded and watched him walk, reluctantly, from his car, parked on the circular white pebble driveway, to her ultra-modern two-storey on a cliff overlooking the mouth of the harbour.

"Only if someone throws them back," she said.

"It only takes one from someone who wants to get even."

He saw the nervous way her hands kneaded her arms. When he reached the front door, he smelled the booze.

She led him into the house. An attractive woman, she was fifty-one, but with enough money to buy back a few of those years at health spas and hair salons. She was quietly dressed in brown skirt and beige blouse, never fashionably loud, not for as long as he had known her, not even with the important positions she held.

They sat in the living room in black leather captain's chairs that swivelled one-eighty to take in the spectacular view. Halifax's skyline was to one side, ocean to the other. In between, the opposite coastline opened to a rosary of villages strung together on a winding black road.

"Are you doing all right?" he asked.

"Just fine," she said. "I'm doing just fine. What about you?"

"I'm getting by."

She chuckled. "Maybe that's what I should have said." She crossed her legs at the ankles. Uncrossed them. Fidgety hands.

"A couple of weeks since him dying is not that long," he consoled.

She leaned her head back and stared at the ceiling. She lowered her head. "You didn't come to Tim's funeral."

"Too many politicians and mucky-mucks," he said.

"Same old Peterson."

"Yeah, same old Peterson."

"How many years?"

"A long time."

"Remember when you used to throw me off your grandfather's dock, and Tim would dive in to save me?"

"I remember a lot of things, Ray. One of them I tried to forget."

She glared at him. "You didn't need to bring that up."

"I know," he said, and gestured at the swanky house, "but it levels the playing field."

She folded her hands at her chin and studied him. "Do you think I called you here just to play a game?"

"Out of the blue, after how many years?" he said, playing it cagey.

"Maybe I was ashamed to call sooner."

"Being friends with a damaged cop, not your style."

She avoided his eyes, inhaled deeply, and slowly blew out the breath. "I didn't know who else to call."

He laughed. "The four of us always together as kids. High school. You and Tim rise to the top. You the socialite with the winning smile, and Tim the silver-spooned socialist with the big cigar. Working the backrooms. Jerry runs off to the army. Which left me. The handyman doing your yard work."

"Maybe I never should've called."

"Maybe you're right."

She shifted uncomfortably. "If it makes a difference, it's not just for me."

"No?"

"It's for Tim too."

"Tim is dead."

"For his memory then. Britney has disappeared."

Peterson played his cards tight. "How long?"

"Three, no, four days. The police told me this morning. They came here."

"What did they say?"

She shook her head as though shaking off the question. "We haven't spoken in years. Tim was the caregiver. He's always been the caregiver."

She pointed out the window at an osprey hanging above the water. "She never came to me, not for anything," she said.

They watched the osprey dive.

"Do you want something to drink?" she asked.

He nodded. "Coffee. Black." He was still watching the osprey. It had a fish in its grasp.

"Nothing stronger?"

"It's still early."

"It never used to be."

The osprey flew out of view. He turned and watched her cross the room to an oak-panelled mini-bar, where she made a Keurig coffee for him and a highball for herself.

No, it never used to be too early, he thought. Drinking too much, too often. On the job, then double shifting so as not to go home to a house of cards.

She returned with a mug and the mixed drink, which he doubted contained very much mix. She handed him the mug and raised her glass. "I shouldn't, I know, but . . . losing Tim . . . and now this. I don't want to think. I don't want to feel."

"I know."

"I know you do." She forced a smile. "This is awkward, isn't it?"

"Not for me. I lost a wife; you lost a husband. And now we both have daughters to worry about. It's like old times." The coolness in his voice hardly camouflaged the hurt.

She faced the ocean view. "It's like she's trying to hurt me. She's still blaming me the same way Katy is blaming you."

"This is not about you, Ray. It's about your daughter."

"And her father. It's about him too."

She sipped the highball. Still looking out the window. Swirled the drink with her index finger. She took another sip.

"I was always the hardliner," she said. She turned to him. "You know all about that."

He did not answer. He drank the coffee without taking his eyes off of her, watching some of her upper crust flake off.

"I came in second," she grumbled, looking into her drink. "Tim sometimes teased me by saying that. Not to be mean. He was never mean. He said it . . . I think he said it because he thought it would make me proud that he cared so much for . . . our daughter. I almost said 'his daughter.' Freudian slip. What do you think?"

Again he remained silent to let her talk.

She took a big sip as though she needed it. "That time at the Marriott was one big mistake."

"I know."

"I got drunk. Did a few lines." Her voice sounded almost venial.

"Let's not play the innocent," he said. "That time in the Marriott was the one that got out of hand."

"You don't think I know that?"

"It wasn't pretty, Ray."

She sipped her drink. "You never told him."

"Telling him would have broken his heart."

"It might have been better that way."

"What makes you say that?"

She sighed, and placed a hand on the window as though to steady herself. "Massive heart attack and he's suddenly dead." Anger crept into her voice. "I couldn't go into his office. I couldn't sleep in our bed, not without him. We shared a closet, and I cry every time I go in to get dressed. You've been through it. You know what it's like."

"It wasn't like that for me," he said, and looked out the window, his lips squeezing on the lie he had told. Then he looked at her and laughed wryly. "When we were kids, high school, I looked up to him. I wanted to be like him."

She groaned and turned away. He could see by her quivering shoulders that she was crying. He held up his hands in a helpless gesture. "What do you want me to do?"

She waved a hand beside her head as though signalling him to give her time.

He shuffled in place.

Raylene stopped crying and turned to him. "The police asked me about her friends, about her boyfriend. I haven't met him. I know his first name is Jeremy, but that's all I know. Do you think he did something to her?"

Peterson avoided answering. "What else did the police ask about?"

"About the work she was doing. I don't know what the hell she was doing, except that she was hounding her father about something. Calling him constantly. Calling his office. He wouldn't talk about it. He wouldn't even look at me."

"Did you tell the police that?"

"Why, for God's sake? Tim's been dead thirteen days. How could he have anything to do . . . ?" Her voice caught and she waved for Peterson to follow her.

They crossed the room and went up three steps to Tim's office, which had an upscale, ultra-modern, high-tech look. There was a kidney-shaped glass-topped executive desk, rightly positioned to view the coastal scape through one glass wall and the open ocean out the other. Centred on the desk were a MacBook Pro with its cover open, and an iPhone. A swivel chair had more levers and knobs than the body had contortions, and over its back hung Tim's light brown sweater with darker brown elbow patches. In the chair arm was a control panel for lights, heat, window blinds, and a Bose stereo system with small wall-mounted speakers.

She stood to one side of the doorway with her left hip leaning against a glass-topped credenza. The ice clinked in the glass, and he turned and saw the way her body trembled, and how the lines around her eyes and mouth had deepened into a pained, frightened look.

"Hit the space bar," she said.

Peterson stepped forward and did so. The laptop woke from sleep mode to Tim's homepage of the Halifax *Chronicle Herald*. On the wall behind O'Connell was a seventy-two-inch monitor, and on its screen flashed the latest edition of the newspaper's front page. In the bottom right corner was the headline "Missing Journalist."

"Tim used to say the local headlines defined the day in politics," she said.

He scrolled the story to a graduation photo of Britney Comer. He had seen a similar photo on a wall in Comer's home office, beside her framed King's College diploma.

"There's a Dropbox file," O'Connell said.

He double clicked the icon for Dropbox. Inside was an email. It was from Britney Comer to Timothy Comer, dated two weeks ago, the day before Tim Comer had died. Peterson opened it.

I believed in you. I trusted you. You are the reason for the good in my life. Now this. Please tell me why. I need to know why. I need to hear it from you.

Peterson turned to see O'Connell drag herself from the office. He followed her to the living room, where she was trembling against the wall of windows. He reached for her arm and she stiffened under his touch. He took the glass from her hand and guided her to one of the swivel chairs, where she sat and wrapped her arms around her shoulders. He dropped to one knee beside her and waited. To him, her glazed brown eyes seemed to have gone inside herself.

Then she pointed at the glass in his hand. He went to mix her another drink. By the time he returned, she had somewhat settled. He handed her the highball, pulled the other chair close to her, and sat.

"You ready to tell me?" he asked.

She shook her head and held up a hand. She took a few sips, settled herself, and looked at him. Her mouth moved on words with no sound. And then the words found voice.

". . . something I had to do, to close his online accounts. I'm his wife and I still wasn't allowed, not without passwords. We didn't share those things. I didn't go into his office and he didn't go into mine. I received a court order that allowed me access. It was awkward going through his things, his papers, his computer files. I called Barbara Dur, Tim's secretary. She said Britney had been pushing hard to meet with her father."

"He wouldn't meet with her?"

"Barbara Dur had strict instructions. But it wasn't until after the funeral that I found out for most of his last week, he hadn't been going to the office." She finished the drink and set the glass down on a side table. "What the hell was going on?" she demanded of him, of herself, of anyone.

He took her hand in both of his. He remembered the Marriott hotel. He had had no warrant for busting open the door to room 427, just her frantic voice on the phone begging him for help.

"Britney left me a phone message a few days ago," he confided. "She said she had good news about Katy."

"Katy?"

"Britney sounded anxious, scared maybe." He decided to leave out the part about Comer's clothes being found not more than a kilometre away. He'd leave that up to Bernie to tell.

It was as though O'Connell sensed he was holding something back, because she suddenly pulled her hands away and stood and stepped away from him. She gripped the chair back.

"After the police left," she said. "I went through all of his emails and his text messages on his phone. They texted each other continuously. But a week, ten days before he died there were no texts." She controlled a sudden urge to cry. "There was something else I found. It was on his desk. Tim must have been looking at it before he . . ." She took a deep breath before continuing. "It was an old photo of Tim when he was fourteen, fifteen years old, standing outside St. Mary's Basilica, where his family went to church. He was holding a Bible."

"Back then he had thoughts of becoming a priest," Peterson said. He got up and stood beside her.

"I know," she said, and turned to the window and watched a container ship steaming out past Devil's Island, a small island beyond the mouth of the harbour. "Because of me he didn't."

"He was glad he didn't," Peterson consoled.

"Don't be so sure of that," she said, still watching the container ship. "If he had become a priest . . ."

"We can't change the past, Ray."

"Just suffer for it."

He saw the tension in her shoulders.

"Was there any truth in all our married years together?" she said, loud enough for him to hear, but soft enough that she could have been directing the question at herself.

They stared at each other, then he asked, "What do you want me to do?"

"What you always do."

• • •

She left the house with a fresh drink in hand and walked the path along the cliff. He watched her from the window. After she disappeared from view, he stood there for the longest time with his eyes closed, head sagging, regretful for having come here, frustrated for feeling that way. Then he opened his eyes and entered Tim's office.

He scanned through computer files. He found only documents related to Tim Comer's work in the Liberal Party. He got up and went to the credenza. On top was a thick file folder, containing newspaper clippings about the premier and cabinet. The clippings had been mounted to thick sheets of paper. He quickly flipped through them, glancing at the headlines.

Mixed among the newspaper clippings was a copy of an

environmental assessment report for a resort and marina on the eastern shore. He had seen a copy of this report at Britney's apartment. He turned to the last page and read that the assessment board, for reasons having to do with coastal integrity, fishing rights, and the projected cutting of more than a hundred square acres of an old growth forest, had not recommended the proposal. He frowned on reading that, then folded the report in half and stuck it into a jacket pocket.

He returned to the desk, opened the computer's desktop calendar, and scrolled back several months. Daytimes were filled with meetings with the premier and members of cabinet, along with some backbenchers. Evenings and weekends went to provincial riding associations, and with big shot lawyers, businessmen, and three real estate developers. One name stood out for not having anything to do with politics or business. It had been slotted in for lunch on the last Thursday of every month. Peterson smiled to see the name: Jerry Martin.

Peterson saw where two months ago, after Comer's first heart attack, Comer had begun trimming down his schedule to little more than cabinet meetings, doctor's appointments, and medical tests. Yet Martin's name still made the calendar. Not monthly meetings. Weekly. And the last one was on the day before Comer's massive coronary.

He closed the computer and joined O'Connell as she returned along the cliffside trail.

The wind was in her hair, and the flyaway look reminded him of when they were kids, twelve, maybe thirteen. They had climbed up Moir's Hill, the four of them: Tim Comer, Jerry Martin, Ray, and himself. Comer and Martin were climbing a lone pine at the top of the hill when Peterson had taken Raylene into his arms and kissed her. She had laughed and pushed him away, but he had always known she had willingly curled into his arms and had kissed him back.

"I'm worried and I don't know what I'm worried about," she said as they walked around the house to his car. She leaned forward and brushed his cheek with hers. "I trust you will find out what was going on. And as much as I don't want to know, you will tell me."

CHAPTER
ELEVEN

Peterson waved from across the street, and Jerry Martin skidded his grocery cart to a stop outside Java Blend Coffee Shop. Recycle bags filled with bottles and cans hung off the front of the cart, off the sides, and off the back.

Peterson crossed to meet him. Martin appeared uneasy, edgy.

They moved to the corner to get out of earshot of the foursome sitting at tables outside the coffee shop.

"It's been a while," Peterson said.

Martin rammed his left foot against a back wheel of the cart so it didn't roll.

"Are you doing all right?" Peterson asked.

"Doing good," Martin said. He wore a light brown coat, and his solid frame tightened as though he begrudged the effort to speak. Then he pointed to the cart loaded with bottles and cans. His voice was coarse and bitter. "I'm riding the wave, you know, got the world by the ass. But I'm not alone on the bottom. You're not living the life either. Fucked up. Timmy Comer said the same thing, but not in those words."

"Tim would've said I was neurotic or emotionally disturbed," Peterson said.

Martin stared at him. "Altar boys. Both of you."

"That was his idea," Peterson said. "I was in it for the wine in the sacristy." He smiled.

Martin frowned. "The two of you blessing yourselves every ten minutes, wanting to be priests."

"I wasn't that bad," Peterson insisted.

"Tim turned out a good man, but you? You're down here with me. Only I'm not reaching for it the way you are, like there was some reward. I found out there's no reward for nothing." Martin's body twitched anxiously, and his face looked scared.

Peterson thought about once seeing Martin's mother sitting at the kitchen table in her nightdress and lighting herself up with a bottle of Old Crow. He had felt ashamed seeing her like that. He had felt sorry too.

"No punishment either," Martin continued, voice rising. "That's the problem. The punishment has to be there. The things I saw. There was no punishment for them. And nowadays there's no punishment for nothing. Explain that."

"I can't explain it," Peterson said calmly. "But it's not something to get worked up about. I'm here to visit, have a talk."

Martin looked at him. Confused expression. "Some things, you know," he said. "They happen. Me ending up like

74

my father, a vet who saw too much and drank too much. No way around it. In the genes. And Timmy being whatever he wanted to be. His father, Mister Moneybags, but that wasn't how he made it to the top. Tim was smart. He should've known better than marry that bitch. But Tim was a good man. He was just good inside."

Peterson caught the bit about Raylene O'Connell, but let it go. "You were smarter than all of us," he said. "You just didn't get the grades to go with it."

"Don't butter me," Martin grumbled. "I know what I am."

"I'm just . . ."

"Fuck you," Martin stormed. Then he looked around at the foursome sitting at the outdoor table. He hefted a bag that hung on the side of the cart and was throwing the cart off balance. He changed its position with a bag on the front. "My old man used to beat the hell out of me too. I hated him the way you hated yours, and the last thing I wanted was to end up like him. I joined, and for what. I came home to what? Nothing."

"I know."

"You don't know. Not like Tim." Martin shrugged with a painful look, as though the past still hurt. "No handouts, but if he could manipulate things . . ."

"You kept him busy for a while," Peterson said.

"I just wanted to drink and do drugs, to stop from thinking . . ."

"It doesn't help, though, does it?"

Martin looked at him. Pointed to his head. "I see them all the time."

Peterson nodded.

"Not just at night, but all the time."

Again Peterson nodded. "They sneak up."

Martin grimaced. Then he lowered his head and gritted his teeth. Martin started shaking, and his face contorted into the look of someone Peterson did not recognize.

"Take it easy, Jerry. Deep breaths. C'mon, in and out. We're here in Halifax, on North Street, old friends shooting the breeze."

It took a while for Martin to clear his head, then he slapped the handle of the grocery cart. "They shoved us aside as though nothing happened there."

"I know. I know, but don't think about it. C'mon, be cool, okay."

Martin nodded. Shrugged. He calmed down a little. "Tim said most of us walk a path we shouldn't be walking. I'm walking nowhere and pushing this goddamn thing. Five days a week for twenty, thirty bucks a day. It's not easy. You try pushing it. Give it a push."

"I don't have to push it, Jerry."

"Just once. I want you to know how hard it is pushing this goddamn thing."

"I know how hard it is."

"You don't know." Martin's voice started to climb again and his face flushed. "You think you know, but you don't. C'mon. Push it."

Peterson stepped behind the grocery cart. Martin had to separate two of the bags at the rear so Peterson could squeeze between them and grip the handle. He had to use his legs to overcome inertia and get the cart rolling, but once it was in motion, pushing it was not that hard.

Martin followed. "Now make a turn."

Peterson did as ordered. Turning the heavily laden grocery cart required him to use his entire body.

"Pushing uphill is a son-of-a-bitch," Martin said. "And this city is nothing but goddamn hills."

Peterson stepped away from the cart and Martin slid behind it. He looked at Peterson.

"I see you around a lot. You see me. I know you see me, but you don't stop to talk. Big shot detective."

"I stopped now."

"Yeah, you stopped now. Feeling guilty, or something?"

"Guilty for what?"

"You know what I'm talking about."

"No. What are you talking about?"

"You can't make up for it."

"Make up for what?"

Again Martin became angry. "You stopped being friends with me, stopped being friends with Tim, and now he's dead."

"I never stopped . . ."

"Tim told me what happened. You needed something done, and Tim wouldn't do it. He said Raylene didn't want him to because helping you with that jam you were in might look bad for him and her. You had some heavy shit coming down for shooting that guy. And then your daughter blowing a tire on the drug scene, and then your wife. Tim wanted to, but that goddamn wife of his . . ."

Peterson cringed. He jockeyed for position. "You and Tim must've talked about a lot more than me."

Martin calmed down. "Yeah, sure. Sports. Hockey a lot. But Tim liked talking about old times, about us growing up and being friends. Not to show me up or nothing. Never strutting. I think he came around because those days were good for him, too, maybe better than being on top."

"Why's that?"

"C'mon, you know as well as me that Timmy Comer was all show. A room would light up when he'd walk in. But that wasn't him. Remember when the three of us would get drunk, and he'd start bawling about being ashamed for who he was?"

"That was Tim talking through a bottle of Mateus."

"Not a chance," Martin said. "That was Tim letting it all hang out. He said a lot of the same things when he'd take me to lunch. He'd take me to nice places. I was dressed like this, but he didn't care. Bottom line, we were friends. Tim never could figure why you dropped out."

"You went to lunch with Tim the day before he died," Peterson pressed.

Martin seemed distracted by the bags on the cart.

"Tell me about him not being happy," Peterson said.

"Did I say that?"

"Pretty much."

Martin shrugged. "Maybe he had too much. A big shot giving him grief, applying pressure."

"What kind of pressure?"

"The kind that squeezes you at both ends."

"And what kind is that?"

"Always the cop."

"I can't help it. The training."

"I was trained too."

"I know you were."

"Peacekeeper." Martin pointed to his head. "Blue helmet. Fucking joke. Doing what? Doing nothing. Counting bodies."

"What else did you and Tim talk about?"

Martin gave a crafty smile, as though someone had just told him a secret. "It's like you think I'm not all there. Catch me up like that. But I know my place, Peterson, I know who I'm loyal to and who I'm not."

"Who are you loyal to, Jerry?"

"Not her. Not fucking her." Martin leaned over the grocery cart. "I get the feeling you're looking for something."

"I am."

"You going to tell me?"

Peterson shrugged it off.

Martin stiffened. "Tim Comer came through when I was a basket case. He helped me hold it together. So yeah, he came around a lot. Talking. Opening up. So if there's anything . . ."

"I found out there was something going on before he died," Peterson said. "I want to know what it was."

"Or maybe she does," Martin said. "You were always her stooge. You had the hots for Raylene, always did."

Peterson held down what he was feeling. Twenty years old with a crush he couldn't crawl out from under, knowing she had looked at him the way he had looked at her, but knowing she had wanted the top rung, and to get it she had to follow the money. He knew other things about her too.

"Tell me about Tim," he said.

"He talked a lot about the life we bury."

"The life we bury?"

"He said he'd buried his life in politics and that now he was changing that."

"What change?"

"A different direction. He called it getting back to basics, searching for something more."

"More than what he already had?" Peterson said.

"Don't put it on, Peterson. You know the feeling when something inside is missing. He didn't have to see the body count, but he saw something else that emptied him out."

"What did he see?"

"Ask his wife?"

Peterson shook his head. "She doesn't know."

Martin pretended to adjust the load on the cart.

Peterson scanned the street. Then he asked, "You know about his daughter?"

Martin continued adjusting the load. "Yeah I know," he said. He stepped back from the cart and poked out his chin. "She was everything to him."

"She wanted to talk to him," Peterson said. "A story she was working on. Political."

"What are you saying?"

"I'm asking you, Jerry. Did Tim ever say anything about his daughter wanting to talk to him about a story she was working on?"

"How should I know?"

"You met with him the day before he died."

Martin stared at him with a puzzled look.

"There was something going on," Peterson said. "I'm not sure what. Ray asked me to look into it."

"And sweep up anything before the cops find out."

"What could they be finding out?"

"Nothing, not with Tim Comer."

"It must be something. You wouldn't have—"

"I don't know where the hell you're coming from."

Martin took out a pack of smokes from the left hip pocket of his jeans, tapped one out, and fingered it thoughtfully.

"Tim talked to me because he knew I was the wall," he said, his voice climbing. "He knew what he said didn't get past me. Now he's dead, and the way he made me feel, I'm never going to feel it again. I don't like saying what I already said. I don't know shit when you come right down to it. And maybe what I know, I already forgot. So stop pumping me. I got a load to cash in."

He stuck the cigarette behind his right ear and put his shoulders and legs into moving the cart.

"If you remember anything. If you want to talk." Peterson called after him.

Martin raised a hand and waved it as though waving him off. He kept going.

CHAPTER
TWELVE

"The Battlefield," the cops called it, the kind of well-armed neighbourhood in which nobody sees anything, and when they do see something, they can't remember what it was they saw; where security locks would just increase the odds of broken windows and kicked-in doors.

Peterson turned onto Caldwell Street and saw Jonathan Hillier's silver Lexus parked in front of a two-storey with police tape around the perimeter. He swung behind the Lexus, got out, and did the slow police walk to the driver's side. Hillier lowered the window and forced a lame smile that accentuated his sleepless eyes and haggard face.

Peterson tapped on the roof. "You always did ride in style."

"I made enough," Hillier said. He chinned the dilapidated house across the street. "Look where it got me."

"Not your fault," Peterson reassured him.

"Yes it is. Get in."

Jonathan Hillier was a disbarred criminal lawyer who had represented drug lords, street-level dealers, and crooked businessmen who were turning profits on the drug scene.

As Peterson opened the door to the Lexus and settled beside him, Hillier asked, "How'd you know I'd be here?"

"When I was looking for my daughter, you were looking for yours. Same rat's ass buildings and crack houses."

"Pushed to the limit," Hillier said. His hands played over the steering wheel. Sparkler on his left hand pinky. Black hair stain covering the grey. "Your daughter still making calls?"

Peterson canted his head toward Hillier.

"At least she's alive," Hillier said.

Peterson shifted uneasily.

"A cop found my daughter's body curled up in a closet with the door open," Hillier said. "A nutcase taking revenge, shouting some shit then opens up with an automatic. She was the only one that didn't get out."

"I know," Peterson said. "And two months don't make it any easier."

Hillier's eyes filled.

Peterson reached out his left hand and gripped Hillier's arm. When Hillier regained his composure, Peterson took back his hand.

"I know what I did," Hillier said. "Defending scum. Living the life and loving it. The money." He snorted a disappointed laugh. "I'm banging whose wife, whose girlfriend, I don't care. Whores and crackheads doing me to get them off a charge. Roll them in the back seat. And the whole time my daughter, yours too, out there on the street fucking for

83

what they can get in their arms or up their nose. What the hell kind of fathers are we?"

Peterson didn't answer.

"At least you cracked heads," Hillier continued. "Me? I went to court for the ones selling them that shit. I'm making a buck. Eating gourmet and riding in style. I deserved what I got. Witness tampering for Christ's sake. I thought I was above the law, like half the goddamn legal eagles earning six figures."

"Two chopped down to one," Peterson said.

"I should've done ten."

"Short time is hard time when you're soft in the belly," Peterson said.

Hillier looked past him to the darkened crack house. "The good life, the fucking good life," he said. "That's what you say when you're living it. But deep down you know that's not what it is. You want it to be, but you know it isn't. Go where you want, do what you want. Money to burn. Then your world rattles apart, goddamn it. You see it for what it is — a birth cord and an urn full of ashes. Tell yourself that enough times."

Peterson looked hard at Hillier. He watched a car drive by, a VW Golf. He looked ahead at the cars parked on the street, then shifted his eyes to see out the back window at the ones parked behind. A man wearing a flat newsboy cap walked the sidewalk weaving in and out of pools of street light. Peterson faced forward and stared at the windscreen. "You can't give in to it," he said.

Hillier held his eyes, then smiled to change the channel. "You're looking for something."

"The cops are investigating a pile of clothes found below

the look-off at Herring Cove," Peterson said. "The clothes were laid out to look like a body. They were covered in blood. A wallet with ID was in the sleeve of the sweater."

"Convenient," Hillier said.

"A set-up," Peterson said. "Last night a snitch handed me a cell phone that went with the ID in the wallet. The last two calls on the woman's phone were to me."

Hillier looked perplexed.

"The calls came from Britney Comer."

"The circle just got smaller," Hillier said.

"You remember."

"Of course I remember. She blew the whistle on Andy Benson."

"I'm the one she told."

"I know, and then you walked him into a compromising situation."

"Rumour."

"Entrapment, Peterson, which was something I could never figure out. You knew Britney and Katy were running Benson's errands to high rollers who didn't want to get their dope from the gutter."

"Tough love," Peterson said, and regretted saying it the moment it was out.

"It got your daughter nowhere," Hillier chided. "He did six months on her turning Crown witness, and she earned a week's worth of life lessons from the wrong people."

"Two days."

"Like it matters. "

They fell silent. Then Peterson said, "Comer turned her life around, became a journalist."

"I knew that."

"She left me a message that she had good news about Katy."

"And you don't trust the chance of receiving good news about your daughter."

"Comer's voice was hesitant, scared," Peterson explained.

"Are you thinking Andy Benson?"

"Good possibility. It could also be the stories she was working on, one about prostitution and another one with a political connection."

Hillier breathed a laugh. "And never the twain shall meet. Dealers and pimps don't like interference, and politicians don't hold journalists in high regard."

"Comer's been missing for a few days," Peterson said.

"Bad sign."

"The cops think so too. I think the political story has to do with her father."

"I forgot about him being a big shot. His wife, too, right?"

"She wants me to find out about the political connection."

"Bury what can be buried is what you're saying."

Peterson didn't answer. It was strangely similar to what Jerry Martin had said.

"What connects you to them?"

"We grew up together. Remained friends, sort of."

"I would never have taken you for walking with the rich and powerful. But then again, we both have a closet full of skeletons. I can ask around. Anything else?"

"We're back to Andy Benson," Peterson said. "I think he wants to pick up where we left off."

"Entrapment again." Hillier smiled.

"I think he has someone following me. I heard he was talking grudge match."

Hillier laid his head on the headrest and thought for a moment. He turned to Peterson. "I can help you with Benson. In fact, I'd be happy to. He's been a screw-up since the day he was born. His older brother, Toby, is nothing to write home about either. The two of them are a mix of bullshit and air freshener."

Peterson knew the book on Toby Benson, one scam after another. Always passing himself off as a class act, with bureaucrats and south-end socialites buying it. Provincial tax credit schemes for made-for-television movies, music concerts, a government cruise ship. He was the older brother, the brains, the conduit to the respectable part of town for his younger brother's porn sleaze and white powder.

"Six months wasn't enough for Andy Benson," Hillier continued. "Lose the look. If I had my way, he'd be doing twenty years for just living."

"Changed man?"

Hillier shook his head. "Same spots, a little faded. I once consulted on assault and sexual assault charges against Andy Benson. Not all that proud that he walked on both of them." He smiled. "I wouldn't mind getting him off the street."

Hillier reached past Peterson to dig in the glove compartment. Peterson saw the SIG Sauer 9mm. Hillier found what he was looking for and showed it to Peterson — a key to a Sargent lock set.

"Last night Benson sideswiped a cop car on Connaught Avenue," Hillier said. "Nothing serious. But a good look in his back seat turned up enough blow to rack up thirty-six months. A good lawyer will chop that in half, and by the time Benson gets sentenced, he'll do community service."

"And you don't want that to happen," Peterson said.

"Slip this to the detective investigating the drug charge. It has to look like the cops found it in Andy Benson's apartment, in his car. It doesn't matter."

"A key to what?"

"Back door to the basement of a warehouse two blocks from here. Don't ask what's inside."

Peterson knew Hillier had made a career by working off the same rule — Don't ask, Don't tell, Don't know.

"I made deals," Hillier said, as if reading his thoughts. "All the time I protected myself. I had this key cut after I did all the paperwork on Benson buying the building. A bargaining chip if it ever came down to that. All the cops have to do is get as broad a warrant as they can get, something like searching for goods obtained from the proceeds off drug trafficking."

Hillier made a supplicating gesture. "Get the key and the address into the right hands, and with what you already owe me for past favours, and for this new information you want, I'll wipe the slate. Who knows, I may not be here to collect at a later date."

"Are you going somewhere?"

"Thinking about it." Hillier pointed at the glove compartment. "I started making travel plans." He turned toward the dilapidated house.

Again Peterson reached and touched Hillier's arm. "You should talk to someone," he said.

"I'm talking to you."

"I mean someone who can help."

"Is it doing you any good?"

"I'm working it through."

"Yeah, but are you getting anywhere?"

Peterson took back his hand. "Pretending to. I have a shrink, and a group therapy thing. Sometimes I talk to a priest."

"Looking for forgiveness?" Hillier waved his hand in the sign of the cross. "Did he absolve you of all your sins?"

Peterson shrugged and opened the car door.

"What's the price on forgiveness?" Hillier challenged. "Is it something I can afford?"

Peterson closed the door and walked around to the driver's side. Hillier lowered the window.

"What do you want me to say?" Peterson said. "That guilt doesn't clean up easy?"

Hillier looked away and grunted something. He looked back at Peterson. "Hell is what we deserve, isn't it? Are you in on the Benson thing?"

Peterson rapped his knuckles on the roof of the car. "The time comes you want to trade this in, give me a call."

"I'll put it in my will," Hillier said. He held up the key. "Are you in or out?"

Peterson took the key, then pulled out his notebook and pen. "What's the address?"

CHAPTER
THIRTEEN

Peterson was curious to know what was inside the basement at the address Hillier had given him. He drove a circuitous route to shake anyone who might be following him, then parked on a side street near the rear entrance to the Seahorse Tavern. One fifteen a.m. and the place was still abuzz. Music blaring. Patrons singing. Laughing. From his kitbag, he grabbed the Maglite and latex gloves, and from under the driver's seat he removed a cat's paw, a twelve-inch steel nail puller. He slipped off his brown field coat to a dark blue hoodie underneath, shoved the nail puller up the sleeve, and rotated the claw part to catch on the inside of the cuff.

He got out of the car and walked to the front of the tavern where a guy, midtwenties, hung over a low railing and was vomiting. A young woman, also drunk, stood by trying to comfort him. The heavy-duty bouncer filled the doorway, watching them.

The wind chased a plastic grocery bag along the street and fetched up against a concrete planter on which a scraggly looking panhandler sat. Peterson approached, and the panhandler held out a Tim Hortons coffee cup. In a jokey voice he said, "For ten bucks, I'll show you where they hid the money."

Peterson knew the voice. Benny Stokes, a down-and-outer who had worked Peterson's side a couple of years back. "For twenty you'll tell me who stole it."

Benny smiled to be remembered. "Double it and I'll take you to where the bodies are buried."

Peterson held out his hand and Stokes shook it.

"You're not around that much," Stokes said.

"I took time off to live a little."

"Doing what?"

Peterson shrugged. "This and that."

"So what brings you down here now?"

Peterson recognized Stokes's question as one of interest in Peterson and the possibility of acquiring information he could sell.

"More of the same," Peterson responded. "I heard you had a job."

Stokes laughed. "You're checking up."

Peterson sloughed it off. "Doing what?"

"Waste Management," Stokes said. "I'm a garbage collector."

"That's what I used to call being a cop."

"At least being a cop paid the bills," Stokes said, and held up the coffee cup to emphasize his point.

"I also heard you have a girlfriend."

Stokes's face fell. "Yeah, but not for long. She has bone cancer."

"Jesus, Benny, I'm sorry."

"Me too." Stokes tried to smile through his feelings. Instead, his face became sullen, his voice edgy. "We got married. Just when you get something going good, God comes and takes it away, like He's jealous or something. Can't stand to see someone happy."

"Anything I can do?"

"Pray."

"I doubt He'd listen to me."

"Well, He sure as hell ain't listening to me. If He is, then He's coming across with the opposite of what I pray for." Stokes's face squeezed with hurt. "If there isn't . . . What the hell is there?" He looked down at the cup with a handful of coins inside.

"I don't know what to say," Peterson said. He looked back at the guy still hung over the rail. The woman was no longer standing beside him. He reached for his wallet, but Stokes shook him off.

"The respect is more than enough," Stokes said.

For an instant, Peterson's blunder hung between them. Then he held out his hands as though offering contrition. "How about I do what I have to do, and we grab a coffee?"

Stokes shook his head. "I've been away from her too long as it is."

Peterson watched Stokes as he moped off, watched him until he rounded a corner, watched him with a pained expression.

● ● ●

There were no surveillance cameras on the front or back of the building, and no alarm decals on the windows and doors. All that might dissuade someone from thinking there was something inside worth stealing were two deadbolts on the steel basement door and two dirt filled window wells.

Peterson had made a call and found out that Andy Benson had made bail and had gone to the casino to celebrate. He was counting on Benson staying there for a while.

He entered the side alley and stood outside the steel door for a moment, listening to neighbourhood sounds. Traffic on the main drag. The faint sound of music from the tavern. Wind chimes from the balcony of an apartment building at the corner. Angry voices from somewhere not far away.

He unlocked the steel door and entered. Upon closing the door, and with the window wells buried in dirt, the room was pitch black. He opened his senses to explore the darkness. The stink of incense. The hurried sound of small scuttling feet. A low unnerving hum.

He snapped on the Maglite and played it around the room. Walls, floor, and ceiling had been painted black. Against the wall to his right was a rumpled queen-sized bed with an elaborate brown-stained headboard with carved scrolls on the posts and a tangle of vines across the panels. In the headboard's centre, almost hidden among the foliage was the coiled body of a snake. Its carved wooden tongue flicked out and its beady eyes stared straight ahead.

He tried the drawers in the black-painted nightstand beside the bed. Empty. So were those in a similarly painted dresser.

There was a narrow, red-painted door directly across from him, and it opened into another room that was like a cavern, which, excluding the small outer room, extended the entire footprint of the building. Steel girders ran the length of it. The walls had also been painted black, except for one, which had two wide horizontal red stripes. At the room's centre were two video cameras similar in size to those he had seen in a television news studio.

Against one wall was a long table with a computer and multi-channel audio mixer. This was the source of the hum. There were speakers at either end of the table. Standing upright on the far wall was a strange looking contraption with a series of ropes and pulleys. Dangling from the ends of four of the ropes were high quality handcuffs.

He examined the contraption. Tugged on a couple of ropes and saw the centreboards pull apart in opposite directions, vertically and horizontally. He recognized it as a rack on which a person's body would be stretched.

The same wall had been fitted with six black-painted hooks. Each held whips of various lengths and of various styles: leather snake whips, braided floggers with multiple strands and knots on the tips. One of the snake whips had a metal barb at the tip. Another was studded the entire length with two-inch thorns.

A shelf on the same wall contained a plastic cylinder of multi-coloured zip ties. Beside it was a loaded Smith & Wesson .38. There were three ringbolts in the wall with the horizontal red stripes. Leather straps hung from each.

He untied one of the straps and chafed a finger over the rough leather. Thinking. He looked at the whips then retied the strap on the ringbolt.

He played the Maglite over the ceiling and saw a small lighting grid directly over the wall with the ringbolts. The black floor sloped to a drain at the centre of the room. He knelt and examined one of several discoloured streaks that ran to the drain from each of the ringbolts.

He followed two video cables from the cameras to the computer and saw a feed from the computer into the audio board, and into the speakers. He hit the space bar. On the screen appeared the still frame of a naked young woman curled on the floor beneath one of the ringbolts. Her right hand was pulling at her brown hair. Her eyes were wide open, terrified. Her mouth stretched into a silent scream.

He thought he recognized the woman, but with her face so contorted, he could not be certain.

He tapped the space bar again, and the woman's long, drawn-out scream suddenly filled the room. He shook at the sound of it. Quickly he reached for the volume control on the audio board.

Then a naked man, with his hairy back to camera, stepped into frame. He was carrying one of the whips Peterson had seen hanging on the wall, the snake whip with two-inch thorns. The man had a slight build and a shaved head. He turned to camera. He wore make-up to look like a scary clown. He grinned, and Peterson felt as though the man was daring him to keep watching. Despite the make-up, Peterson recognized the man as Andy Benson.

The young woman whimpered, and Benson turned and softly whipped her. Then he whipped her harder and harder, the thorns scoring her flesh and drawing blood. She screamed and writhed on the floor under what had now become vicious blows. The blood flowed freely. She crawled toward the camera, staring into the lens and screaming. The video ended abruptly.

Peterson stared eerily at the black screen. A sound escaped his throat, and it surprised him. He became aware that his hands were clenched and his mouth was dry. He dragged the cursor on the timeline of the video to the still frame of the young woman screaming, where it had been when he arrived.

When he reached his car, he realized where he had seen this woman. It was a little more than a year ago. A photograph in the *Chronicle Herald*, a twenty-one-year-old missing person whose body had been found half buried in a sand dune near Fox Point. Broken ribs. Broken nose. Eyeholes blank. No suspects. No one was ever charged. Her name was Leanne Bobbitt.

CHAPTER
FOURTEEN

No granola, no whipped cream and fruit-laden waffles, and no smoked salmon and avocado salads. The world-beaters and limousine socialists could go somewhere else. Reggie's Place served the everyman all-day breakfast seven days a week — eggs your way, bacon, ham, sausage, burnt toast for the hangover, French toast for the savoir faire, and strong coffee, plenty of it. Reggie's was a block and a half from the police station, and was a regular pit stop for those going on or coming off shift.

Peterson sat at a corner table with his back to the wall. Behind him was the large mural of Reggie's first operation, a food truck. He stared at nothing, the night before still clawing inside his head.

Angie set an order of burnt toast before him and topped up his mug of black coffee. She had rouged cheeks and starving eyes, and wore a blue tunic with yesterday's stains. He looked up at her.

"You hear about my cousin?" she said.

He shook his head and cradled his mug of coffee.

"He owns a fencing business, puts up metal fences. He has a contract to run one along the 104 to keep the deer off the highway."

"He must be doing good," he said.

"He is. A week ago someone broke into his storage yard and drove off with a truckload of metal pipe."

Peterson looked past her to the front window as though he were waiting for someone.

"He caught the truck on surveillance video, but no licence number, and too grainy to see the make and model. The cops said there's not much they can do."

Peterson drank his coffee.

"Nothing they can do, huh?" Angie emphasized. "My cousin made the rounds of scrap metal outfits and at one of them there's a truck unloading his pipe. Does he call the cops? Not on your life. No offence, Peterson, but that would've gotten him nowhere fast."

He looked at her.

"He called his two brothers who work for him," she continued. "They made the thieves reload the pipe into their truck, then beat the hell out of them. You ask me, that's how justice should be done."

He went at the coffee. She moved on to another table.

Two uniformed cops entered and ordered coffee and western sandwiches to go. They nodded to Peterson. One of them came over and asked, "Do you miss the front line?"

"Not everything," Peterson said. "There were some parts that were good."

"I know the feeling," the cop said. "I got divorced two months ago. Now I'm missing the upside of being married. Crazy, isn't it?"

Peterson nodded and drank his coffee.

Ten minutes later Detective Jamie Gould, gelled hair and permanent grin, joined Peterson at the corner table.

"Good to see you," he said and held out his hand, damn near shaking Peterson's arm off.

"Careful, Jamie, they'll start calling you a head case for playing nice with me."

"Political correctness, my friend. Eccentric is the worst it can get. Even with refusing an office and working out of the coffee room, I'm still not the wild man you used to be."

"Don't believe everything you heard," Peterson cautioned, holding up his mug to Angie for a refill. "I'm on the outside looking in."

"Yeah, but what a ride before they kicked you out."

Angie came over and refilled Peterson's mug. "You must drink a gallon of this stuff a day. I don't know why you don't get the runs."

She turned to Gould. "You eating?"

"Toasted bagel. Strawberry jam. I hope I don't get the runs."

She scowled, filled his mug, and left.

"You caught the Benson case," Peterson said.

"A friend of yours?" Gould joked.

Peterson drank some coffee.

"He's a work of art," Gould continued. "Rich guy with a chip. Has a sheet as long as your arm. Minor league stuff. Possession. Public intoxication. Three dropped charges for sexual assault. Drunk driving. It goes on and on. Does whatever the hell he wants. What's your interest?"

Peterson dug into his pocket for the key and a slip of paper with the warehouse address written on it.

"You didn't get this from me," he said, and slid both across the table.

Gould didn't blink. He put them in his pocket. Sipped his coffee.

Peterson waited for the young couple at a nearby table to shoulder their backpacks and make for the door.

"It opens a basement door in a warehouse in the Battlefield," he said. "Holding companies owning holding companies. Short story is the building belongs to Benson. Start with the paperwork and get a warrant."

"I have him on drunk driving and possession of enough blow to qualify as trafficking."

"Go for the proceeds of his criminal activity."

"A judge might call it a fishing trip," Gould proposed.

"Do whatever you have to do to get inside that basement legally."

"How'd you find out about this?"

"That's not open for discussion."

"How do I explain the key?"

Peterson tried not to show his frustration. If it were Danny Little, back when they had been partners, there would be no need for explanation.

"Get forensics to find the key in his car, and don't use an anonymous source."

Gould grinned. "What am I looking for?"

Peterson shook his head, frowned. "You won't like it."

"If it puts this bastard away, I will."

"No, you won't."

CHAPTER
FIFTEEN

Peterson carried a coffee to a bright red Adirondack chair outside the Central Library on Spring Garden Road. He sat with his back to the building, eyes on the move, scrutinizing the rush-hour flow of pedestrians passing in front of the library and jamming up at the traffic light at the corner of Queen Street and Spring Garden.

A few minutes later, Bernie showed up with a coffee and a snack box of Timbits. She passed Peterson the coffee and box to hold while she carried over a yellow Adirondack chair and sat beside him. She yawned, then tilted back her head and closed her eyes.

"Not good," he said.

"Four a.m. call. Homicide." She offered him a Timbit.

"How many's that in one week?"

"Like they're falling out of trees," she said, and popped a Timbit into her mouth, chewed, and washed it down with coffee. "A forty-two-year-old white male with a ten-inch carving knife in his chest, and a woman's in the bedroom screaming it was an accident."

He reached into the box for one of the Timbits.

"It takes a lot of effort to break the breast bone," he said between chews.

"Especially for a woman who goes a hundred and twenty pounds at most. Danny and I figure he was on the floor already, and she came onto the knife with all her weight. Some accident."

"Why was he on the floor?"

"Drunk probably. We got nothing from the woman. A post-mortem should answer a lot of questions."

Bernie saw him scanning the street. "You looking for someone?"

"Just a feeling of being followed. I've had it for the last few days. Spotted a blue Ford Explorer a couple of times. Once was when I met you out at Herring Cove."

"Following you?"

"It could also be a coincidence."

"We both know better than that," she said.

He shrugged.

"An old flame, or someone new with a crush?" she asked.

He prayed his hands together under his chin, and looked out at nothing.

She saw his mood change and said, "The holes we get ourselves into."

He looked at her. "We?"

"One big goddamn mess," she said

He helped himself to another Timbit.

"The big shot south end philanthropist who bludgeoned his son to death six weeks ago . . ." she said.

"Harrison. Cut and dry, I thought," he mumbled with a mouthful.

"I wish. The deputy chief compromised the crime scene."

Peterson swallowed hard. "What the hell was Fultz doing there?"

"He wants the top job when Menard retires," she said.

"If he retires," Peterson said. "He was supposed to do that two years ago."

"Maybe he likes the limelight," she said. "Fultz sure does."

"Ass-kissing his way up the ladder." Peterson scowled. "Stepping on others to get there."

"You in particular," she said.

He shrugged.

Bernie said, "He must've thought a little publicity in a high-profile case would up his chances for the chief's job. He was standing in the middle of the room when Danny and I stopped him. No booties. No gloves. Nothing. Blood everywhere, on the floor, desk. And Fultz was touching this and that, walking around. His assistant was taking pictures for God's sake."

She offered him the last Timbit, which he refused.

"I can see it coming," he said.

Bernie nodded. She ate the Timbit. Drank her coffee. "Danny agreed to let it go, say nothing to no one, not forensics, not the Crown."

"And you?"

"What am I supposed to do? If Danny goes along and I

don't, it's my career. And not just me, Richie Leighton was on the door when Fultz bulled his way in. Leighton's only three years in uniform, if he doesn't play ball, he's working mall security."

Peterson cringed at the situation she and Leighton were in. "Danny won't listen to me," he said, discouraged.

"That's not why I'm telling you."

They both scanned the street, letting the silence have its time. Then Bernie said, "I'm keeping Comer's mother up to date on our investigation."

Peterson did not respond.

"I get the feeling the mother doesn't like her daughter's boyfriend."

"Most parents don't, not at first. Wait till your son comes home with a girl. You'll run her name through the system."

"Did you?"

"Katy never brought them home, and I wasn't there even if she did."

"Comer's mother mentioned your daughter, and she mentioned you. About something you did for Britney. We're following up on Britney's contacts list. Friends and family. Danny's looking into the boyfriend. We're also checking out the father."

Peterson felt her watching him.

"Tim Comer is dead," he said.

"Even important people make enemies."

She drained the coffee, then stuffed the cup into the empty snack box, and set it on the ground beside her. "You know the mother, right?"

"You know I do. And you also know I went out there to see her."

105

Bernie tilted her head quizzically.

"A visit from two detectives sends signals," he said.

"Shouldn't matter if she has nothing to hide."

"We all have something to hide."

"Some have a lot more than others," she said. "You were friends with her husband too. "

"We all grew up together."

"Friends in important places. Is that how you skated past all the trouble you made for yourself?"

He met her eyes. "When you reach the top, friends on the bottom can look very small."

"Then why did she call you?"

"She wants me to find out what I can, protect her daughter's good name, and her husband's. I suppose that means her own as well."

"I hope that doesn't mean cover-up."

He winced. "You didn't say that, did you?"

"The way things are going these days, maybe I did."

His face saddened. "If I find out anything that incriminates anyone, you'll be the first to know."

"Tell me about him," she said.

He waited before answering. "Born rich, born smart, and born into a political family. His life was measured out from day one."

"Ambitious?"

He nodded. "But not ruthless, not for all the years I've known him."

"Her boyfriend said she was working on a political story."

"And one on prostitution, and another about the Food Bank," he emphasized.

"Yeah, but her father was a politician. Maybe he knew something."

"Tim Comer played the backrooms. Never out in front. Never gave interviews."

"Not even with his daughter?"

"Not if it would put her life in jeopardy."

"Do you think her life's in jeopardy?"

"She's been missing how long? You know the stats."

Bernie pulled out her iPad and took notes on what they had already discussed, then swiped back a few pages. Read those notes. She said, "There's nothing else. A few things Danny doesn't want me talking about, not yet, not until we know more."

"But you're going to tell me."

"No I'm not. You're holding back something about Comer. I'm holding back some of what I have."

"What makes you think I'm holding back?"

"Gut feeling. Like the one I got when Danny told me your daughter was up on a drug charge, and that the charge was dropped when she turned Crown witness."

Peterson looked uncomfortable. "Then he told you the rest of it too."

"He did."

"They were underage, Bernie, rebellious teens seeking romance in the forbidden fruit."

"That's a quaint way of putting it. Does it make you feel better about yourself?"

He looked away from Bernie to across the street, where a woman sat at a table outside a Turkish restaurant. But Bernie waited.

His body sagged into the chair. "I suspected something like drugs for a while," he said.

"And you did nothing about it?"

"I tried. I locked her in the basement. That didn't work."

"So she bolts and starts living on the street, making friends with all the wrong people."

He rolled his tongue inside his lower lip.

"Then Britney snitched to you about what was going on," Bernie challenged. "Danny said you wouldn't even post your daughter's bail. He did."

"I thought the justice system would do her some good."

"She was your daughter. She didn't need punishment, Peterson."

"I was wrong, all right?"

"She needed you being there once in a while. It's not all them. Parents have a lot to do with how their kids turn out."

He squirmed. "That's what my wife said."

"She was right."

"Yeah she was right," he grumbled, and offered an excusive shrug. "It was a time when I wasn't playing my best game. It got so I didn't want to bring the job home."

"A lot of cops finish a shift and don't bring it home," she protested.

"Name one who pulled the trigger on someone and still leaves it in the locker."

Bernie turned away. Took her time. "That wasn't fair, was it?"

Peterson sloughed it off. "Yeah, it was fair. I wasn't much of a father. And I wasn't much of a husband."

She let it go, then said, "Taking off the badge at night doesn't change who you are. It doesn't make me like myself any more or any less. And right now, with all that's going down, I don't even know if I like being a cop. Non-stop on the job. Walking into my son's classroom and sizing it up. Suspicious of everything and everyone. I got here and read your inventory right off. I saw you weren't carrying."

"Not in the last year," he confessed, holding out his arms like wings, as though offering himself up to be frisked. "I don't want to do something stupid, not again." He gripped the chair arms and closed his eyes, as though not wanting her to see what he saw.

They fell silent for a while, then Bernie said, "I still think you're holding something back. But I'll give you something else. A biologist at the Bedford Institute of Oceanography, a university friend of Britney Comer's, told her about an environmental study that went sideways. Danny's talking to him right now." She drew in her legs and got up. "I have a meeting at my son's school tonight."

"How's he doing?"

"His teachers think he needs counselling."

"And?"

"No father, and a mother who works a lot."

"And you tore a strip off me," he griped.

"I don't like it any more than you did," she said. "And sometimes I wonder if I'm right for what I do."

"You're good at it," he offered.

"Yeah, sure." She fell silent for a moment. Then she said, "Maybe this Harrison fiasco is a good reason to get out. I'm up to here with shovelling shit against the tide. What about you?"

Peterson got up to go. "A favour for a friend's sister," he said. "I have to return a laptop to its rightful owner."

"Always the knight-errant."

"Yeah, well, some guy, a university professor who likes sex the hard way, he needs a talking to."

CHAPTER
SIXTEEN

The professor lived in the lower flat of a two-storey on Edward Street, near the university, a neighbourhood that was a mix of faculty offices, student flats, and frat houses.

Peterson leaned heavy on the doorbell. When that didn't deliver an immediate response, he hammered on the door. A porch light flicked on and the door opened to a middle-aged man in blue-and-white-checked pyjamas. He had a midforties spread, tonsured head, and a tentative, wispy smile. Hardly the look of a stud who went in for whips and black leather.

"Are you Walter Barlow?" Peterson demanded, playing the heavy.

Barlow could barely get out a yes.

"I want to talk to you."

"To me?" Barlow said.

"Can I come in?" Peterson pressured. "You don't want your neighbours knowing your business."

Barlow stepped aside, and Peterson found his way to the living room, which was lined with floor-to-ceiling bookcases. Books were also stacked on an upright piano, and on the piano bench. Others were in piles of twos and threes around a plaid-patterned couch and around a grey overstuffed armchair. Peterson sat on the couch. Barlow remained standing.

"What's this about?" Barlow asked.

Peterson gestured for him to take a seat in the armchair. Then he set the laptop on a thick pad of paper, which was on top of an oak and marble coffee table.

"You like dirty pictures," Peterson said.

Barlow looked from the laptop to Peterson. His narrow face was a mix of confusion and fear. He reached for the armchair and lowered himself into it.

"You like more than dirty pictures," Peterson continued.

Barlow stared at him.

"You like whips and bondage, and I'm guessing from the website I can't open that you like a lot worse things that you don't want anyone to see. You like being a tough guy, too, beating on a woman because she wouldn't play hide-and-seek."

Barlow squirmed and struggled to speak. "I don't know what you're talking about."

"I'm talking about Ellen Doyle."

"I don't know . . ."

"You beat her up."

"Beat her up?"

"That's what she says."

"My God. I have a girlfriend, I'm not that . . . And I don't know this other person . . ."

"Ellen Doyle."

"Why would she say that about me?"

"What about the sex club you wanted her to join?"

"What?"

"A sex club. Kinky top to bottom."

Barlow was stunned. "I don't do those things," he whined. "You can't be accusing me of something like that."

Peterson nudged the laptop toward Barlow. "It's on the laptop you left at her place."

Barlow looked at the laptop, then at Peterson. "That's not mine." He reached under the coffee table for a black Samsung laptop. "This is mine."

"Then why would Ellen Doyle get a peace bond against you?" Peterson said.

Barlow ran his hands through his thinning brown hair. "I don't know anyone named Ellen Doyle. What are you doing to me?" His eyes were tearful and his mouth pinched tight as though holding back a groan.

"You are Walter Barlow?" Peterson confirmed.

"Yes."

"An English Prof?"

"Yes. But I've done nothing like what you said. I wouldn't hurt—"

"She gave me your name, your address," Peterson said.

"But it's not me," Barlow insisted.

"Why would she say it was?"

"I don't know why."

Peterson didn't think Barlow was the aggressive type, not the kind of man who would smack Ellen Doyle for not joining his sex games. Mistaken identity? Not likely. It was someone else — either a different Barlow, or someone else entirely.

He retrieved the laptop from the coffee table and got up to leave. When he reached the doorway, he turned back and saw Barlow sunken into his shoulders, his face cupped in his hands. "I'm sorry, Mr. Barlow," he said and opened the door.

Barlow looked up. He shook with anger. "You belittled me, and for what?" His arms fell helplessly at his sides. "I don't know what's going on."

"Neither do I."

Peterson drove two blocks and pulled over. Thinking. Shaking his head at the confusion of it all. After several minutes of sitting in his car in front of a row of upscale homes, he called Ellen Doyle.

"It's noisy," he said.

"I'm downtown, Durty Nelly's," she said. "Where are you?"

"Tell me what Barlow looks like."

"You know, long hair, in between all right–looking and just all right." She gave a drunken giggle.

He swallowed hard and hung up. "Goddamn," he said out loud, and shifted into gear.

CHAPTER
SEVENTEEN

Peterson waited until the evening news had finished, knowing she'd still be at her desk, seldom in a rush to go home. She'd hang at the station for a couple more hours. Make notes on news stories she was not happy with; maybe tear a strip off the graphics department for lousy weather maps, or off a cameraman or sound person for missing her cues. She sought perfection, and that made her one of the best at what she did. It also made Terri-Lee Norton a very difficult person to work with. As a reporter, before she became news director, Norton and Peterson had had a working relationship. Each had squeezed the other for inside information.

Always with her shoulders back, grim look, and convincing handshake, which left the recipient without doubt that she was all business. Yet, to Peterson, there was something attractive about her commanding presence. Midfifties. Stylishly dressed. Brown hair, going grey, which suggested she was no fool about the aging process. She wore very little make-up, again signalling others that she was in control and unashamed of her age, which both intensified her no-nonsense news director's attitude and subtly complemented the plain, simple beauty of her face.

"What's this to you?" she asked as she led him through the soundproof door to the control room and into the newsroom. A skeleton news crew were at their computers. Her office was out of the question. She didn't want him seeing anything she didn't want him to see.

"A childhood friend of my daughter," he said, a little too rehearsed for his liking.

"And that's enough to get you back in the game?"

He let that one go.

"Always the hard-ass in the cop shop, and now you're going private detective," she scoffed, and pointed for him to take the anchor's chair at a desk with the newsroom in the background.

"Not likely," he said,

"Then what do you call it?" Norton asked.

"A hobby."

She laughed and rolled up a vacant chair from a nearby reporter's desk.

"I expect you have something to trade."

"Not at the moment."

"A futures deal doesn't play well with me."

"This will."

She looked into the overhead grid of studio lights. Spoke to them. "Did you hear that, Lord? Should I give him one more chance before I kick him out on his ass?" She lowered her head and looked at him.

He waited for two, three, four beats. Then he held up the thumb drive of Britney's voice message and enticed, "A recording of what may turn out to be her last words."

Norton suddenly stiffened at being caught off guard. "How the hell did you get that?"

"Source protection," he said, pleased at the opportunity to say that to a journalist.

She didn't like hearing it any more than the justice department did.

"Always the smart guy," she said.

"You mean for a has-been?"

"Is this your sensitive side? How nice."

He replied with a forced smile.

"When do I get it?" she demanded.

"That's something you have to trust me with."

"Trust!" The word was like a trumpet blast, and the handful in the newsroom looked up from their computers to see who was getting the sharp end of Norton's tongue.

"Yeah, trust," he said softly. "You want the definition? Late-night anchor caught in a public washroom with his pants down."

She rolled her eyes. Crease for a smile. "A female detective was here this afternoon."

"I know about the Food Bank story. Now tell me what you didn't tell the detective."

"Just so we're clear: I get the recording and your end of the story before the cops do."

"Unless you don't tell me something more than I already know."

Norton pursed her lips and made a kissing sound. "She was working the Food Bank, getting somewhere, I thought. Then she came in with something else. A prostitute who had gotten beaten up, you know, a porn film that got out of hand. No news in that. But the porn film angle did interest me. Lots of visuals. Tease viewers with the story on our newscast, then send them to our website for more in-depth coverage. So I told her to work the Food Bank story, and if she found out more on the other, we could talk again."

The technical director for the late-night news, a bearded, heavy-set man who walked with a slight limp, came over to where Norton and Peterson sat. He reported to her about readjusting a bank of lights on the weather set and asked if she wanted to have a look before he knocked off and went home.

Norton asked Peterson to wait for a minute, then followed the technical director to the control room. Peterson heard her ranting before the soundproof door had whooshed closed behind her. Five minutes later she returned. Face flushed.

"Porno film," he said to remind her of where she had left off.

She acknowledged his reminder and regained her seat. Then she ran her hands upward along her cheeks to the top of her head and down again. She did that three times, each time twisting her head back and forth. To Peterson, it looked as though she was trying to screw her head back on. She dropped her hands into her lap and leaned forward.

"They forced you out didn't they?" she said, and studied his reaction.

He tried to make sense of why she was asking that. "Disability pension," he said.

"Not your choice, was it?"

"What does this have to . . . ?"

"I'm just asking."

"No, it was not my choice."

"So you found a hobby that suits you."

"Some things fall my way, and I do what I do."

"I can't imagine it. If I'm not directing news, I don't know what I'd do."

Peterson sensed that she wanted to talk. He said nothing.

"I know what I am," she said. "I also know how good I am. But this day and age, good isn't good enough. They want me to be less belligerent. One union grievance after another. You know what I'm talking about."

He did not respond.

"Twenty years ago you didn't fire Nerf balls to break the glass ceiling," she said. "We shot lead pellets. Now? A psychiatric exam."

She threw back her head and stared at the overhead grid. She looked at him. "What were we talking about?"

"Britney Comer and a porno film," he said, pleased to have gotten back on track.

She nodded in such a way as to suggest that she didn't know if she wanted to continue talking to him or not.

"I thought porn was too much for her to handle," she said. "I wanted the Food Bank item. Timely copy I could run whenever we had a hole to fill. But Comer wanted something with more meat. So I told her to work both, but I insisted the Food Bank had precedence. It must have been a week, ten days, and she comes back. This time she says she has something juicy that involves top government officials, maybe the premier and friends."

"Related to the porno film?" he pressed.

"I don't know. Maybe. She said it was hot and it was big, and that she needed a cameraman to help document the story."

"And you kept this from the cops," he said.

She shrugged. "They had nothing to offer." She looked away from Peterson, cracked a disappointed smile then turned back. "She was pushy, and I didn't like a freelancer, especially someone fresh out of school, coming in here and getting pushy. I told her I'd give the story to someone who covered politics. If there was something solid to what she had, then I would bring her in on it." Norton crossed her arms at her chest as though in self-defence, or perhaps defiance. "If it really was big, I didn't want her screwing it up."

Peterson waited for her to continue.

Norton harrumphed, then said, "She walked out. If she thought . . ." Norton fell silent for a moment. When she did speak, her voice was low, almost contrite. "Maybe if there was someone with experience working with her."

"Maybe," Peterson said. "Are you thinking porn or politics?"

"Is there a difference?"

"Porn is a lot more violent."

"Are you sure about that? I'm not. You work in this business, start shaking bushes, you get a lot of backs up."

"Try being a cop."

"We ask a lot of the same questions to a lot of the same people. And we ask questions to people cops never get to ask them to." Again she ran her hands up her cheeks to the top of her head and back again. This time she didn't twist her head about. "I shouldn't have encouraged her," she said, and thought for a moment. "I said I didn't like pushy, and I don't. But I liked it in her. A few years of experience, and Comer won't be firing Nerf balls. I hope you're wrong about 'last words.'"

"What was the political angle?"

"I don't know."

"Yes you do." He held up the thumb drive as a reminder.

She smiled. "She said there was a paper trail. She wouldn't tell me more than that. She didn't want to lose the story to someone else."

"And you didn't want the cops ruining a good story," he said.

"There's no story until I see documented proof."

"Did Comer seem worried?"

Norton shifted uncomfortably in the chair. "That's why I wanted someone with experience to handle it."

CHAPTER
EIGHTEEN

Stephanie Zola's cramped office was on the ground floor of a two-storey office building, which had long been destined for the wrecking ball. Peterson tried her office door, but it was locked, and there were no lights on inside. He then looked for her in the downtown hangouts, where she would pass out pamphlets to working girls, offering them the opportunity to turn their lives around. He came up empty.

Then he cruised a north-end stroll and saw a woman leaning against a concrete apartment building, dragging on a smoke. Her name was Crystal Bungay. Her street name was Buffy. She had played snitch for him in the past. He pulled over under a street light, and she approached the car after he lowered the passenger-side window. She leaned in and, at seeing him, rolled her eye-shadowed dark blue twenty-three-year-old eyes.

"You buying it now," she said, and slung back the brown jacket to reveal a pink tank top.

"You know better than that," he said.

She straightened her jacket.

"You need a coffee or something?" he asked.

She faked a smile. "What's the something?"

"Toast. Bagel."

She looked across the street. "I got a living to make."

"I'll pay for your time," he said.

He drove to a coffee shop that shared space with a rock-climbing wall and grabbed a table overlooking the street. Buffy sat opposite. Fidgety hands. Lacing her fingers to quiet them down. When that didn't work, she went to the ladies room. He went to the counter and ordered coffee for them both, and a toasted and buttered bagel for her.

Buffy returned, her eyes high-beaming like she was in the zone.

They took a moment to size each other up, each using their own learned experience to sight-read the other. Her face was full of dark grey mornings. He just looked sad.

"You look good," he lied.

"For being messed up, right?"

"That's not what I said. You look better than the last time, that's all."

"When was that?"

"When you were in a bar downtown and . . . causing trouble."

"Am I supposed to thank you?" Her hands now rested easy around the coffee mug.

He shook his head. "Ever think about where all this is going?"

She gave him a sourpuss. "Don't you people ever get tired of asking? I got no education, Peterson, and a kid to feed." She looked around the coffee shop. "I could be begging change on Spring Garden Road. No worse, I could be hustling doughnuts and coffee for ten an hour. And you know where I'd be? At the food bank or diving dumpsters behind Sobeys."

"Not if you didn't blow the money up your nose."

She threw him a tight smile. She held up her arms to surrender. "I tried going straight," she said. "After two months without painkillers, I was back on the street." She pointed at the twosome halfway up the wall. "Cut me off, and you want to see someone climb. This is my life, Peterson."

She ran a finger through the butter on the bagel then licked it. She looked at him. "I need at least fifty bucks for the time I'm spending." She drank her coffee.

He nodded and said, "I'm looking for Stephanie Zola."

"You investigating or something?"

"Or something."

"I haven't seen Zola in a while. No one has."

"Since when?"

"Since I don't know. Five days, maybe."

"Where was that?"

"Outside the Horseshoe. She was doing her thing, passing out pamphlets. Then that journalist shows up, and they got in a car."

"Was the journalist Britney Comer?"

She nodded as she drank her coffee. "She's a friend of Zola's."

"You know that she's gone missing," he said, and watched Buffy turn away. Frightened eyes. Staring at the street and the passing traffic.

She nodded. "That's why you're asking about Zola." Her eyes were now fixed on the bagel. "She came around a couple of times with Zee, asking too many questions."

"About what?"

Her voice went cold. "About screwing for money. She was writing something. I wouldn't talk to her."

"Why not?"

She shrugged and finished her coffee. "I heard some things," she offered.

"Like what?"

"Things. You work the street, you hear things." She reached for a napkin from a dispenser on the table and wiped her nose. "I know what I do, Peterson. Forgetting a lot of things is part of it. And not talking out of turn is another."

Peterson thought about it, then asked, "Did you see the driver of the car they got into?"

She bit into the bagel.

"Then what about the car?"

"I don't know cars," she said through a mouthful. "It was one of those SUVs. Blue."

Peterson held down his surprise. "And you're sure you didn't see the driver?"

She licked butter off the bagel.

He drank his coffee. Recognized he had hit a dead end.

"Any street talk about Zola getting back in the business?" He let that question sound nonchalant, as though it had just occurred to him.

"Not Zee," she replied.

"Not even porno?"

"That's a game for underage prosti-tots," she said. "Go online and check it out. The perverts want to watch virgins get it for the first time, or girls young enough to pretend they're virgins. Twenty-three, and I'm already too old. Zee is way over the hill. She must be, what, thirty maybe? Talk to Leechy Murphy. He's her half-brother. He kept her safe when she was working the street."

"Where do I find him?"

"At night, he could be anywhere. Late morning, afternoon, he hangs at that place where they throw axes."

"The Timber?"

"Yeah. He's a pain in the ass, you know. Plays tough. He did some time, for what I don't know, so maybe he earned the right to be a shithead." She finished off the bagel. "We got to go," she said. "I pay a guy to keep an eye out. We stay longer, and you're running into a hundred bills."

He finished his coffee. Then he drove her to where he had picked her up. She opened the door to get out. Then she poked her head back into the car.

"There was a woman in the passenger seat," she said.

"Yeah?"

"Yeah. She turned to say something to Zee and the other one. I seen her before, I don't know, three or four, maybe five years ago. She was hustling for whatever she could score. Strung out. She looked like she was still that way."

"You still remember her?"

"Yeah. The cops had come around showing me her picture, made me study it, you know, like she was important. She was fifteen, maybe."

"That would make her nineteen, twenty now," he said.

"She hasn't changed much. Zee recognized her too. I could tell from how they talked. I don't know, you know, the way their bodies moved. Hands."

"Like they knew one another?"

"Yeah. From before."

He thought about it. Then, as Buffy started to withdraw her head from inside the car, he halted her.

"Wait a minute," he said, going to his back pocket for his wallet and fumbling out a photograph. He reached it across the car for Buffy to see.

She looked at the photo and then at Peterson. She nodded.

CHAPTER
NINETEEN

He often went to the cemetery to think. He sat in the darkness on a headstone opposite his wife's grave. His elbows hung over his knees, head down. He was still sitting there thirty minutes later when, at 3:07 a.m., his phone buzzed a text message. Unknown number. He opened it. The message read: "Watch this!"

There was a link embedded in the text. He thought it was from his daughter, and at that moment he wanted some contact with her. He clicked on the link. It opened to a video of a wall with broken plaster and lath poking out. Multi-coloured horizontal lines had been painted on it. The camera panned left along the horizontal lines to a frightened Britney Comer sitting in a high-back chair with her wrists tied to the chair arms. She was draped in what looked like a pale green shower curtain, with yellow fish printed on it. Her dirty blond hair was uncombed and sweaty looking. She was talking to someone behind the video camera.

"My name? Britney Comer," she said.

"Tell me about your childhood," a man's voice encouraged.

"What?"

"Your childhood, tell me about it."

The camera tightened to a close-up of her face, which was stretched with incomprehension and fear.

"Your childhood, Britney. Tell me about it."

"I . . . I don't know. It was normal."

"How was it normal?"

Her head tilted down, and she started to cry.

"Crying won't help," the man said. "Talking will. I want you to talk to me."

Britney tried to stop crying. She looked at the camera.

"How was your childhood normal?"

She sniffled, her voice weakened. "I went to school, played with friends."

"Did you have many friends?"

"Not many."

"You had best friends, I'll bet."

She nodded. The shower curtain slipped from a shoulder and partially revealed one of her breasts.

"Who were they?"

"My best friends?"

"Yes. Tell me about your very best friend."

The video cut to a grainy photo of two little girls in a playground. They were in close-up. They were eight or nine years old, standing in front of monkey bars with their arms around each other's shoulders and smiling into the camera.

Peterson trembled to see the photo. One of the girls was Britney. The other was his daughter.

"My best friend was Katy," Comer said.

"What was her last name?"

The video cut back to Comer tied in the high-back chair. "Peterson," she said. "Katy Peterson."

"And you were best friends?"

"Yes."

"Are you still best friends?"

"No. No."

"When was the last time you saw her?" the man asked.

The video cut to a clip of a woman being brutally whipped by a man with his back to camera. The man wore jeans and a red plaid shirt. His hair fell to his shoulders. He raised his arm, flung it forward, and the whip violently snapped on the woman's back. Again, and then again. In voice-over, Comer was saying, "Today. Yesterday. I don't know. I don't know how many days it is."

Peterson caught his breath. He recognized the woman being whipped as Stephanie Zola.

"Of course you remember," the man said. "When was the last time?"

The video cut to Comer tied in the chair. But the soundtrack of the whipping continued in the background.

"Yesterday," she said.

A vicious scream punctuated her answer. Then the video of Comer cut back to the photo of the girls in the playground.

"What happened to your best friend?" The man's voice asked.

"She moved away."

"Where did she move to?"

"Vancouver."

"That's so far away," the man mocked. "Why did she move to Vancouver?"

The video cut to a close-up of Comer in the high-back chair, her face like wrinkled cloth. "A man. He was stalking her."

"Stalking her?"

"Yes. It was the same man . . ."

"The same man?"

"Yes," she squeaked. "The one who . . ."

"Tell me about the man."

Comer started to cry.

Slowly the camera zoomed to an extreme close-up of Comer's mouth. Lips parted. Teeth clenched. Sobbing.

"I told you to stop crying," the man insisted. "Now tell me about the man."

The video slowed, accentuating the shape of the words on Comer's lips. She was saying, "We were delivering drugs for him, and he raped me."

Slowly her mouth widened into a long drawn-out howl. Then the video resumed normal play as the man's mocking voice said, "Raped?"

Comer keened and sobbed.

The man broke into a maniacal laugh. Then he commanded her to stop crying.

Comer tried to stop. Couldn't. Tried again. Whimpering.

The man said in a voice suffused with malice, "You told on him selling drugs. Now he's coming here."

Comer howled, and the video cut to black.

Peterson stared at the iPhone. Swallowed dryly. His breathing had quickened.

Then the phone rang. He held it to one side so as not to look at it. Frightened to answer it. But he did.

The same man's voice said, again in that sneering tone, "Mother and Wife, In Loving Memory."

This was the inscription on Peterson's wife's headstone. He scanned the darkness to see who was watching him. He saw only the shape of trees, and moonlight reflecting off the granite markers.

"How banal," the man said. "But then your marriage was banal, wasn't it? Fatherhood banal too."

"Who is this?" Peterson demanded.

"Did you watch the video?"

Peterson didn't answer.

"There's more to it," the man said. "Drugs. Rape. An accomplice turned Crown witness. What was her name? What became of her? You know, I know you do. Tell me a story, Daddy. Tell me a lie. Tell me how you protect other girls but you don't protect me."

There was a long silence in which Peterson stood repulsed by his own presence. His eyes flared. From the corner of his tightened mouth squeezed a drop of spit. His knuckles puffed. Glumly he clamped a hand over his eyes.

The man's voice whispered, "Do you remember the story of Little Black Sambo? I'm sure you read it to Katy when she was a little girl."

Peterson dropped his hand and cringed to hear the man say his daughter's name. He knew the book, but said nothing in response.

"It's a children's story that is anything but childish," the man continued. "After giving his colourful clothes to four hungry tigers, to stop them from eating him, Sambo climbs a

132

tree to escape. The tigers are vain. Each wants what the other is wearing. So they chase each other around the tree, faster and faster, until the tigers run so fast they turn into butter. Then Sambo climbs down from the tree, gathers up the butter, and brings it home to his mother to make pancakes."

The man laughed, and the sound of his laughter crackled like static.

"What do you think, Peterson? Is the story a metaphor?"

Again Peterson remained silent.

The man said, "Think about it. Their flesh and blood, and their self-contained energy churned into something life-giving like butter. A miracle so to speak. Like bread and wine. Is that what this is all about? I wonder. I wonder so many things. I wonder if people scream to help quiet their pain. And when they scream, does God even hear them? Does He hear their prayers? Does He hear the tree that falls in the forest when no one is nearby? Does He even care about trees?"

There was a long pause, then the man said, "Unless it is the tree in the Garden of Eden, and we are all racing around it until *we* turn into butter. Or in the garden of Gethsemane. Sweating drops of blood. Is that possible, Peterson. Can a man sweat blood? Or is this also a metaphor? All metaphors. So many of them. Perhaps life itself is a metaphor. Bread and wine into body and blood. And body and blood into melted butter. What does it mean, Peterson? You know. I know you do."

Peterson's voice was throaty. "What do you want?"

The man whispered, "We were three feet apart. He's pointing a gun at my head and I was pointing mine at his. I wasn't breathing. I wasn't feeling. I just wanted to back my way out of there. I wanted to go home to my wife and daughter. Then he moved and I pulled the trigger, and I never wanted to go home again."

The phone went dead, and Peterson stared into the darkness. His hands were shaking. Two days ago, he had said those exact same words to Dr. Heaney.

CHAPTER
TWENTY

The clink of glasses stirred Peterson. He swung his feet from the chair and saw Cotter had been cleaning up the bar, whatever hadn't been done before closing the night before. Without a word to Cotter, Peterson got up and climbed upstairs to Cotter's place to shower and shave.

When he returned, Cotter said, "I hope you used your own toothbrush and razor."

Peterson ignored him, distracted by whatever vision he saw three feet in front of his face.

"You got a key to the place already," Cotter continued. "How 'bout you buy into one-half of The Office? You're in here most of the time anyway."

Peterson went behind the bar, ran the sink tap until the water was cold, and filled a beer glass. He drank it, then turned to the coffee urn. He removed the guts, filled the urn with water, and tore open a packet of dark roast.

"I take it you don't like the idea," Cotter said to Peterson's silence.

Peterson yawned. "How much money are you talking?"

"Are you serious," Cotter said, straightening bottles on a shelf behind the bar. "Because if you're serious, I'm serious. I know you don't know the pub business, but I'll show you the ropes, like I did when you were a rookie cop."

"You showed me paperwork back then," Peterson teased.

"Yeah, but back then paperwork was half the job. Not like now with these computers in the car. I could show you the ins and outs again. And it's not like you have to live in here like I do. You pull a shift. Day, night, I don't care. The thing is I could use an infusion of cash. And a partner would be a blessing, even you."

"Thanks," Peterson said.

"Don't take that the wrong way. We've known one another a long time. I know you're a head case sometimes, but I can live with that. I mean, I'm living with it now."

Peterson waited for the coffee urn to finish perking.

"And you need a change," Cotter continued. "Janice said the same thing. You got to get something going in your life. And owning half of this place won't mean too much of a change. Cops are in here a lot. Old times, you know what I mean. On top of that, we get the odd ones, too, talking the street. You'll feel right at home. Never skip a beat."

"Tell me how much you want, and I'll think about it," Peterson said.

"You're not just yanking my chain. You're serious, right?"

Peterson nodded, and for that moment, he was serious. He circled the bar and sat facing Cotter.

Cotter stooped to reach under the bar for a white towel to wipe his hands. He straightened and groaned.

"There's another thing," he complained. "I'm getting older. Back aches. Knees ache, shoulders ache. What isn't sore is flabby. And there's nothing I can do about it. Time isn't kind to anyone, Peterson. Work out all you want. Colour your hair. Get cosmetic surgery. A tuck here, a tuck there. It doesn't matter."

The red light on the urn flashed red. Peterson grabbed a mug and filled it.

"The clock keeps ticking," Cotter was saying. "People talk half full, half empty. They're all up to their necks in bullshit. No matter what, the glass is draining dry. For me, and for you."

Peterson raised the mug in a toast.

"And even though I got you by about ten, fifteen years, there's got to be less time for you than me. I may be old with knuckles that have me popping pills, but you? You took one in the chest. Like if that bullet hadn't landed two, three inches another way . . . You know what I'm talking about. The regulars in here say it a lot, 'Peterson's living on borrowed time.' They say it like someone can really do that. But then, I want to know who do you borrow it from? It's not like there's a bank you can go to. And if there was, who makes deposits of years off their lives? I sure as hell ain't giving up any of my time. Maybe some twenty-year-old world-beater who thinks he'll live forever would. What about you, Peterson? What would you pay for the guarantee of more time?"

Peterson shrugged, a noncommittal answer.

"Yeah I know," Cotter continued. "I'm talking through my ass. But I'm alone at night and I think about this kind of stuff. You're alone a lot too. What do you think about?"

Peterson looked past Cotter at himself in the mirror behind the bar.

"Seriously," Cotter said, "right now, what are you thinking about?"

Peterson turned to him. "Thinking too much is what got me into trouble."

"Drinking was what got you into trouble," Cotter corrected. "And that was so you couldn't think."

Peterson raised the coffee mug. "What makes you think I'm done with it?"

"Because you've been three, almost four years on black coffee. And I think you hang out in a bar just to remind yourself how bad it can get."

"Still want me as a partner?"

Cotter unscrewed the top off a jug of orange juice and filled a beer glass. "I wouldn't mention it if I didn't mean it." He took a big drink, then changed the subject. "Ziggy was in here again. He wants to see you. He said you're trying to save the world and don't have a chance of doing it. What was he talking about?"

"I don't know."

"Sure you do. You're just not saying."

"Do you think God is a metaphor?" Peterson asked.

"God doesn't play into my life. Why are you asking?"

"A phone call I got."

"Does this have to do with what Ziggy was saying?"

"Possibly."

Peterson told Cotter about Comer's phone message, about her clothes laid out like a body off a cliff near Herring Cove, about the video of her tied to a chair and the voice asking her questions, and about the same voice calling him a few minutes later and talking crazy about tigers turning into butter the way bread turns into the body of Christ. He also told about the voice asking if God was just a metaphor. He held back from telling Cotter about the voice repeating something Peterson had told his psychiatrist in private. He intended to talk to Dr. Heaney about that in about an hour.

Cotter reached behind for a file folder beside the old-fashioned cash register. "You asked me to do some homework," he said.

He opened the folder on the bar and slid from it a one-page, single-spaced police report. Peterson knew Cotter had memorized it; a habit from his cop days when he had been a desk sergeant, a permanent assignment after a car had run a stop sign and ploughed his police cruiser into a corner of St. Joe's Church. He had cut through the boredom by knowing the ins and outs of all the paper that had crossed his desk. Arrest warrants, suspect and victim profiles, court hearings. It had been his way of being on the front line. Feeling important.

"2018, blue Ford Explorer with BC plates and licence number EDP871," Cotter said. "It belongs to David Charon."

He looked at the page in his hand. Looked up.

"Thirty-one years old. Grew up in Nova Scotia. Studied television and film production at Nova Scotia Community College. Worked freelance as a grip in the film industry here until the government pulled the plug and it went tits-up. He went west, Toronto and then Vancouver. A note attached to his file described him as an aspiring film director with little talent. The industry out there blackballed him for heavy drug use on set. That was in 2016. He dropped off the radar after that." Cotter sipped the orange juice.

"Priors?" Peterson asked.

"Five charges," Cotter said. "All in Vancouver. Three for aggravated sexual assault and two for attempted aggravated sexual assault. Apparently the man got into the porn film game. Two of the charges had to do with the bondage and S&M getting out of hand. None of the charges ever made it to trial. The old consensual this and that I suspect. Especially when they both were playing with whips and handcuffs. On three of the charges, there were online videos to support his side of the story. The website was Sexlife." He gave Peterson a crafty smile, as though he were giving away a secret. "Don't give me the eyes. I'm over eighteen." He replaced the page in the folder and handed it to Peterson. "Why is this guy getting you involved?"

"Not sure," Peterson said.

"You must have some idea."

"Only that he's going out of his way to leave a trail."

"To catch what?"

"Who," Peterson said. "To catch who."

Cotter thought for a moment, then asked, "What does God have to do with all this?"

Peterson shrugged, then widened his arms to a gesture that encompassed the entire pub. "You still haven't set a price."

CHAPTER
TWENTY-ONE

Peterson arrived to see the four of them huddled outside the brownstone community resource building.

"She's never late," the grey-bearded guy said, nervously toeing the pavement, his voice half statement, half complaint. "I'm here early, I always come early, and she's always here first."

"So what's going on?" The soldier with the butch cut hair asked Peterson, as though she thought he should know more than anyone else. "What are we supposed to do?"

Peterson didn't take the time to answer. He headed back to his car, made a phone call, and had Dr. Heaney's home address in a moment. When he arrived, there were three police cruisers and the forensics van parked in front of an upscale brown-and-beige two-storey, near Dalhousie University. The neighbourhood consisted of similar-sized houses. Some housed faculty offices, some student residences, and some were private homes. Danny's white Malibu and Bernie's red Chevy Cruz were parked behind the cruisers.

There were two cops on the door, and one of them recognized Peterson.

"Can you tell Bernie I'm out here?" Peterson asked the cop.

"She's up to her eyes right now," the cop responded.

"I have something about what went on here."

"I'll tell her." The cop left his post and went inside the house. A minute later he was back out. "She said give her five."

Peterson waited in his car. But it wasn't Bernie who exited the house. It was Danny. Peterson walked to meet him.

"What are you doing here?" Danny challenged. His voice and face were flushed.

"Dr. Heaney was my psychiatrist," Peterson said and leaned against a police cruiser.

Danny stood his ground and let him talk.

"At three this morning I got a call from a guy who repeated something I had said to Heaney in private, word for word. She recorded our sessions so she could review them. Sometimes she played them back to me so I could think about what I had said, search for the truth in it."

"Why are you telling me this?"

"Because I think someone else listened to those recordings. I wanted to ask her, but she didn't show up at the morning group session. I knew something had happened."

"What do you think happened?"

"What is this, Dan?"

142

Danny gave him an expressionless face.

Peterson sensed what was going on. He pulled out his cell phone. "Let me show you something. The same person sent me this."

He brought up the text message, but when he scrolled to the link for the video of Britney Comer tied to a chair, the link had disappeared.

"What the hell's going on?" he muttered.

"You tell me," Danny said, his voice charged with accusation. "When was the last time you saw Dr. Heaney?"

Peterson crossed his arms at his chest. "Two days ago at a group session."

"Did you get along with her?"

"Jesus Christ, Dan. She's keeping me from doing something I sometimes want to do." He looked past Danny at the forensics team exiting the house and loading their van. "She was making a difference for the four of us. And she was doing it on her own dime. Now what happened to her?"

"Someone was tearing her office apart," Danny said. "She heard them, came downstairs, and they beat her up."

"How is she?"

Danny rose on his toes then lowered back down. "Her chances are good. So if Mr. Mysterious calls again, keep that under wraps."

"He was after my file," Peterson said.

Danny studied him. "Why would someone do that?"

"I'm not sure, but he's been following me."

Danny scowled. "On top of everything else, now you've gone paranoid."

"A blue SUV. Guy with long hair . . ."

"That could be any one of a hundred people wanting to

get even with you. Which doesn't mean any one of them broke in here."

"To me it does."

Danny shook his head pitifully. "Where were you last night?" he demanded.

Peterson's shoulders dropped, and he held up his hands in a gesture of conciliation. "After all the years together . . ."

"You're breaking my heart," Danny said scornfully, and walked away.

Peterson walked back to his car. As he got in, his phone rang. There was a long silence. Then the man who had called him earlier that morning said, "The machete is a Godless weapon." The line went dead.

CHAPTER
TWENTY-TWO

Harold Desgrosseilliers had a contact named Jekyll, a one-time hacker who the Mounties had helped to see the light, a chain-smoking twenty-two-year-old who lived in a duplex on Larry Uteck Boulevard.

"A freelancer," Gross had said with a smile in his voice. "But she's anything but free. Six figures, and the Mounties are shelling out half of what she makes. The rest comes from government departments and corporations with security problems."

"Then I doubt I can afford her," Peterson said, switching the cell to his left hand as he turned onto the Bicentennial Highway on his way to Larry Uteck Boulevard.

"I told her you were former police, a city cop who holds a lot of I.O.U.'s. She said she'd do what she could."

To meet her, Peterson drove off the highway and down Larry Uteck through an ugly swamp of high-rises, which testified to the creative vacuity of architects and real estate developers. At the lower end of the boulevard was a mind-numbing neighbourhood of duplexes, all the same shape and size, and all with light brown vinyl siding.

No handshake, not on Jekyll's part, just a straight smile that conveyed little warmth and a whole lot of annoyance. She was tall and weedy, and wore black stretch pants and a bulky grey sweater. Her short orange-streaked hair framed a narrow face, with eyes that looked out from a gulf that was deeper than her age.

She led him through a living room and dining room, both of which had no furniture, and both of which smelled of cigarette smoke. The window did not have shades or blinds, and the grey light through them added to the bleak-ness of the rooms. As they passed by the kitchen, he saw that it had a pine pedestal table and only one chair, and he thought if the house had not come with a fridge and stove, she probably wouldn't even have them.

They climbed the stairs, Jekyll taking two at a time, and entered a bedroom furnished with a computer desk with two iMacs on top, a large glass ashtray gagging on butts, a swivel chair, and a brown futon. In a corner stood a grey metal rack of hard drives. Beside it was a metal folding chair. Jekyll gestured for him to take that. He opened it and sat beside her swivel chair. She lit a smoke.

"Is Jekyll your last name?" he asked.

"Is Peterson yours?"

"Yeah."

"Do you have a first name?" she pressed.

"I don't use it," he said.

"Me neither."

"Probably for the same reason," he said.

She drew deeply off the smoke and stared at him. "Gross told me what you want. Give me your phone."

He handed it to her.

"Thumb print or password?"

"What?"

"On your phone."

"Password."

"Punch it in."

She held out the phone, and he punched in his password. Then she scrolled to the text message that the voice had sent him and set up a Bluetooth link between his phone and the iMacs.

"It's just software," she said, as she keyed in code. "Like Snapchat, only a little more sophisticated, but not that much."

He pretended he knew about Snapchat, thinking that Gross had been right when the business exec had suggested Peterson was playing detective in a cyber world he knew little about. He watched as she continued. She paired his phone to her iMacs and worked with his phone image on their screens. Her fingers flew over the keyboard, and her eyes followed the cursor.

"Gross said you can hack into anything," he said.

She threw him a look that read his meaning loud and clear. "You have something else?" she asked.

"When you're done with that."

"I'm done." She handed him the phone.

He saw that she had returned the link into the text message.

"You can play it as much as you want," she said.

He opened the link on his phone and the video played to the screens on both iMacs. They saw Britney Comer tied to the chair and heard the man's voice asking her questions.

Jekyll said, "That's creepy. Who is she?"

"A missing person."

"And the guy doing the talking?"

"I think his name is David Charon, a sex offender out of Vancouver."

"And I'll bet he uploads to porn sites," she said.

"That's the other thing I'd like you to do."

She hit the space bar and stopped the video.

"The Mounties have me helping them," she said. "I hack sites. Money laundering, child porn. I try not to watch, but you see things. So the sites you want me to hack, are they more of this stuff?"

"Maybe. It was on the laptop of a guy who beat up a woman because she wouldn't play sex games with him. He gave the woman a different name, Walter Barlow, but I think it was this David Charon. I think he's the same guy as the voice in the video."

He showed her the notepad that had been in the shoulder bag, and opened it to the address of the website.

She read it and looked at him. "Do you have any idea where this will take us?" Her voice was more informed than inquisitive.

"Gross said something about it," he said.

"Watching this stuff changes you. These aren't Hollywood movies. They're sharing videos about some pretty bad stuff. Do you really want to go there?"

Peterson nodded.

She tapped out another smoke and reached for a pack of matches. "If the site is password-protected, it could take time to hack in."

"How long?"

"A while."

"That could mean a big fee," he said.

"Yeah it could," she nodded, and smiled for the first time. "I have a friend serving a one-year sentence in Burnside. He's not doing too well."

"A fellow hacker?"

"A judge wanted to teach him a lesson."

"Stiff sentence. I'm surprised his lawyer didn't appeal."

"He did, but an appeal takes time. My friend doesn't think he can last much longer. The inmates had a go at him."

"The Mounties won't help?"

"I won't ask them."

Peterson hesitated, then gave in. "I might be able to get protection for your friend. No promises."

"Does anyone make them anymore?"

"Not when you see the world for what it is," he said.

Jekyll waved her hand as though waving away something she didn't like. "I'll call when I'm done," she said.

He saw himself out.

CHAPTER
TWENTY-THREE

Later that afternoon, Ziggy sat outside his tin can home in an outdoor rocker looking out at the Fairview Container Terminal and beyond that to the Bedford Basin. Halifax Harbour was like a long-handled spoon, and the Basin was its bowl.

Peterson descended the same gravel path as he had a few nights before. Ziggy turned to his footsteps and cried out, "Woe to you within the grip of evil, for the fire will devour your flesh openly."

Peterson drew close and stood over him.

Ziggy's eyes flashed with fun. "You shall reap tombs of darkness, Peterson, and the fruit off the tree of evil."

"Stuff it, Ziggy. Tell me what you have or I'm out of here."

Ziggy had the bong in his lap and he now took a hit

from it. He exhaled and spoke through his smoky breath, "You do for me; I do for you."

"Only if you have something more than Bible thumping."

Ziggy took another hit off the bong.

"First thing this morning, I mean we're talking early, Peterson. No sun in the sky, and this guy is banging on the side of my box. I stuck my gun in his face and sat him down right here, where I'm sitting now. He had a gift for you. Package wrapped. No bow."

"Where's the gift?"

Ziggy shook his head then opened his hands and stretched them forward in a gesture of benediction. "Give unto others as you would have them give unto you."

"What do you want?"

"It costs me twenty, sometimes fifty, to stay high all day."

Peterson reached for his wallet and laid three tens in Ziggy's open hand.

"Fifty would've been better," Ziggy said.

Peterson breathed a laugh. "Country of compromises, Zig." He held out his hand for the gift.

Ziggy got up with a great deal of effort and entered the metal container. He returned holding a blue Birks jewellery box in one hand and the brown paper wrapping in the other.

"You opened it," Peterson challenged.

"Sometimes the mailman needs to know what he's delivering." He handed box and paper to Peterson. "You do not realize that you dwell in darkness and in death."

On the front side of the paper was Peterson's name composed with capital letters from various printed sources. He handed that back to Ziggy and removed the lid on the box.

Inside was a bloody finger with an emerald green–painted fingernail.

There was a note crammed inside the lid. Peterson unfolded it. It too had been composed in capital letters from various sources: "DO YOU THINK GOD HEARD THE SOUND OF HER SCREAMING?"

CHAPTER
TWENTY-FOUR

The Timber Lounge was a former two-door car-rental service converted into what was supposed to resemble an outbuilding in a lumber camp. Rough wood walls. Tree trunk slabs for tabletops. Wild West saloon–style chandeliers.

Four sat at a table in a side room with a bandstand in a corner. They were watching replays of mixed martial arts fights on a big screen TV. Six more hung in a backroom framed by a four-by-twelve-foot horizontal window in the wall behind the bar. The window was there so those at the bar could watch the action in back. Two of those in back were standing and drinking beer, two more sat on stools at a tall table, also drinking, and two were inside a wire cage throwing double-blade axes at targets ten metres away. In the barroom, one man sat alone near the bar, another at a corner table in the shadows.

Peterson entered and button-holed the bartender, who was doing double duty as a waiter. The bartender was dressed as the urban misconception of a lumberjack: jeans with a black-and-red checked shirt. He had a bloomy face and beer bud cheeks. Drinking the profits.

"What'll you have?" he said.

Peterson leaned toward him and whispered, "I'm looking for a guy named Leechy."

"You're a cop, right?" the bartender said.

"Just nod to where he is," Peterson answered.

The bartender indicated a fat man at the corner table. He had a hangdog face, with his chin in his hand like he was already five weeks into a bad month. Peterson peeled off a twenty, handed it to the bartender, asked for privacy, and joined Leechy at the slab table.

"You want to talk in here or outside?" Peterson said.

The man lifted his head. "Talk about what?" He had beer breath and watery eyes.

"Steppie Zee," Peterson said.

"Who are you?"

"A friend of hers."

"What kind is that?"

"I'm like her Guardian Angel."

"I heard about them in catechism class," Leechy said. "Nothing but a goddamn lie."

Peterson reached for Leechy's right hand and shook it. "Lies don't shake hands."

"So what do you want?"

"I want to know about Steppie Zee."

Leechy shook his head and tried to take his hand back, but Peterson would not let go.

"Let's play a game," Peterson said, sliding his hand to Leechy's thumb and gripping it. "I ask questions, and you answer them."

"What if I don't?"

"Then I break your fingers, starting with your thumb."

"What?" Leechy looked to the bartender, who had been watching them. "He'll call the cops."

"And you'll be drinking with your left hand."

"Jesus Christ. You're crazy."

"You have no idea."

Leechy licked his lips then reached his left hand for the beer he had been drinking and drained it.

"Let's start with Steppie Zee," Peterson said.

"Half-sister. We joke about which half."

"You played muscle when she was working."

"What of it?"

"Still taking her calls? Pimping her out?"

"She ain't working no more."

"Leaves you out. Short on cash?"

"I do all right."

"Doing what?"

"Doing what I do."

"And what's that? Arranging a pickup outside the Horseshoe the other night. Blue SUV."

"Fuck off," Leechy said defiantly.

Peterson cranked the thumb, and Leechy choked on a cry.

The bartender stepped forward, but Peterson stared him off.

"Try again," Peterson said.

Leechy winced to say it. "I got a call. A guy does pornos. He wants that journalist to interview him. He wants me to

155

line it up. He said my sister should bring her, you know, so she would feel safe."

"Why an interview?"

"Like I asked, huh? The guy said two hundred. You think I'm asking questions?"

Leechy looked to the bartender for help, but the barkeep was pulling beers for the axe throwers in the backroom.

"Then what happened?"

"The guy said outside the Horseshoe. He'd send a car. I thought high class. Interview. What could go wrong, right?"

"The two hundred didn't play into your decision, did it?"

Leechy didn't answer.

Peterson pressured the thumb. "Who was the guy?"

"I didn't take a census."

Peterson bent back the thumb.

Leechy croaked then said, "Like someone I don't know about. A phone call. A guy talking in a crazy man voice, saying a lot of dumb-ass shit."

"The bells didn't go off?" Peterson challenged.

"In this business? When I was hustling and Zee working, I used to get them talking like sissies, talking ballsy like they're selling Ram trucks, talking like they're sucking their own thumb. I never gave a shit what they talked like."

Leechy looked at the bartender, who now had gone into the axe-throwing room to deliver a tray of beer. He looked at Peterson. "Come on, ease up."

"Where is Zee now?" Peterson asked, holding tight on his grip.

"No idea. I haven't seen her since outside the Horseshoe. No one has. And don't ask if I called the cops. You know better than that."

156

"Did she call you?"

Leechy shook his head.

"You have her cell number?"

"She ain't answering."

"Give it to me anyway." With his free hand, Peterson reached for the pen in his jacket pocket and wrote the phone number on the back of the hand that gripped Leechy's thumb. He also pressured Leechy for Zola's address. Leechy didn't know the exact number, but said it was the second one from The Tower, heading downtown, nameplate on her door.

"Now Britney Comer," Peterson said.

Leechy closed his eyes for a long time then opened them. "Pain in the ass media. Pushy. I didn't like what she wanted to write about. Stir up shit."

"Like how?"

"Like people and politicians wanting to clean the streets, like we're all nothing but shit cancering up the city. And then the cops come around busting balls. Anyway, I didn't convince her to go. Zee did."

Peterson gave up a smile to disguise his sudden surprise. "Comer didn't want to go?"

"She had something else going on," Leechy said. "Big shot politician or something. There was a video, she said."

"A video of what?"

"It could be him screwing his mother for all I know."

"Did Zee know about it?"

Leechy smirked. "We ain't twins. We don't do that tele-something shit. What she knows and don't know doesn't travel from her head into mine. And she never said one way or the other."

"But she wanted in on the two hundred," Peterson sneered.

"She likes nice," Leechy said. "Always did."

"I saw Zee in an online video," Peterson said. "A goon was putting the boots to her. For two bills, split two ways, it wasn't nice."

CHAPTER
TWENTY-FIVE

He parked outside a green vinyl-sided two-storey, which was the second set of flats south of The Tower on Brunswick Street. Waited. Watched for movement inside. Then he called and let Zola's phone ring through to the service announcement that the customer he wanted was unavailable.

The front hall, unlike so many he had entered in this neighbourhood, was clean and smelled of sticky sweet air freshener. He climbed the narrow stairway to a landing with two doors on opposite ends. One of the doors had a yellow plastic happy face attached to it. The name, Zee, was hand printed across the forehead. From his wallet, he pulled four different-sized lock picks, selected one, and unlocked the door to a neat and orderly three-room flat.

The bathroom was clean and smelling of lemons. The kitchen also smelled of lemons. with just a single plate and coffee mug on the drain board. In the living room there was a set of double-hung windows, with blue flowered curtains, looking out on St. George's Round Church. He opened the bedroom door and saw the bed was made, dresser tidy. Combs and hairbrush lined up and positioned to face forward. Beside them were several bottles of nail polish on a pink ceramic tray. What struck him was that one of them was emerald green.

He entered and sat in a brown cushioned chair beside a red flowered sofa, both facing a wall-mounted thirty-two-inch Samsung. Blue ceramic coasters were neatly stacked on a pine Ikea coffee table. On a matching end table were several black-and-white handouts, with the header "Do It Now."

One of the rose-coloured walls, the one with the brushed white single pedestal desk pushed up against it, had an amateurish painting of red roses in a white vase. On the same wall was an oil painting of two middle-aged men sitting on a green wooden bench outside a restaurant. One of the men was singing; the other sat with his hands folded on his lap, clearly embarrassed. On the opposite wall hung a pen-and-ink sketch of a bearded, naked overweight man sitting on a hobbyhorse and smoking. Peterson thought the oil painting and sketch were pretty good.

He looked around the room and wondered if Stephanie Zola had been as fastidious in her living accommodation when she had been working the street. Then his cop sense settled on the white single-pedestal desk against the wall. No desktop computer. No laptop. No phone.

He went through the three drawers in the pedestal, which turned out to be catchalls for knick-knacks, CDs, two hair brushes, a round tabletop vanity mirror, an LED flashlight, loose AA batteries, a book of *Erotic Love Poems*, and another of *Bawdy Limericks*. Out of curiosity, he opened *Erotic Love Poems* to a page with a folded corner. He read the first stanza from a poem with a checkmark beside it. It was by Robert Herrick.

> I do not love to wed,
> Though I do like to woo,
> And for a maidenhead
> I'll beg and buy it too.

The centre drawer contained the usual assortment of pens, as well as the previous month's utility bill and water bill, and a receipt from City Property Management for two months' rent. There was also a birthday card from Mrs. Pauline Emmerson. On the envelope was a return address for 37 Skyline Terrace, Wolfville, Nova Scotia.

He copied this into his notepad. Then he searched the kitchen cupboards and the drawers in the bedroom dresser and nightstand, thumbed through a stack of women's magazines from a rack beside the bed, and turned out seat cushions on the chair and sofa. He replaced the cushions and sat in the chair. Closed his eyes. Opened them.

He went back into the kitchen opened the fridge and saw that it was well stocked with the usual. On the pine wainscotted wall beside the fridge hung a wall calendar from the Dairy Farmers of Nova Scotia. A closer look at the various penned entries made him smile. He thumbed back through the months and saw similar entries — three different sets of initials beside three-digit numbers. On one of the entries, after the number, was the word *Mari*.

It did not take him long to put it together. Clever girl. Recording her dates not on her computer and not on her smart phone, but on a wall calendar, hanging in plain view. Room numbers. A john's initials. Three regulars. Probably three of them she had valued, and still did. *Mari* for *Marriott*. The other entries must have been for the same hotel, one she had preferred in the past, and still did. No need to record its name.

Counselling prostitutes to give it up. He almost laughed.

He looked for an entry for the night Comer had gone missing. Nothing had been written on that date.

He returned to the living room and sat in the same brown chair.

"Blue SUV," he mumbled to the empty room. "Interview?"

He got up, crossed the room, and sat at the white desk. Stared at the watercolour of red roses in a white vase and muttered, "Where was that guy taking you?"

CHAPTER
TWENTY-SIX

Jekyll sat on her front porch smoking. The laptop Peterson had left with her was on the porch beside her. Peterson parked in front of her duplex and sat on a lower step. Jekyll stared straight ahead, unwilling to look at him. Without a word, she pushed the laptop toward him, as though she was pushing away an unwanted ugliness that had touched her life. A folded sheet of paper and a business card were Scotch taped on top. The business card was for Corporal Jennifer Collins, the same RCMP contact Harold Desgrosseilliers had given him. Peterson put the laptop under his arm.

She pointed at it.

"It's like a game," she said. Gravelled voice. "This person has been uploading to the dark web for over a year. It's all there. You'll see."

She stared skyward and slowly shook her head. Her face was full of sorrow.

She spoke without looking at him. "You should drop that off with Corporal Collins. Let her try and trace the IP address to the owner."

"Probably stolen," he said.

"You never know. I wrote out the username and password, and instructions on how to use Tor to access the dark web and the website."

She looked at him. Gestured at the laptop. "The woman you're looking for? I hope you don't find her in there."

● ● ●

He returned home, unconcerned whether the blue SUV was following him or not. As he passed through the living room to the den, the failings of his life surrounded him. The room was cold and comfortless, with furnishings that looked like they smelled of damp earth.

He entered the den and fired up the iMac, where he was confronted with a new email from his daughter, with three images of a dilapidated farmhouse. One was a view of the farmhouse at the far end of an overgrown field. Maples overhung a rutted, shadowy driveway.

The second image was tighter, taken at an angle to the house, showing a summer kitchen with one of its walls propped up by two long poles. On the wall, in large red letters were the words *Fuck You*.

The third was a full frontal view of the house. There was no front porch, and the door had been boarded up. Boards also covered the upstairs windows. The glass in the ground-floor window had six panes, two of which had diagonal cracks. In the bottom right pane, he saw what looked like a person. He enlarged the photo and saw the blurred image of a woman's face staring out at him.

He enlarged the photo even more, but the pixelated image became indistinguishable.

He pushed back from the desk and thought about these photos, about why his daughter had sent them. In the past, her photos had always been of various filthy rooms with unmade beds and condoms and drug paraphernalia lying about. Why an abandoned farmhouse?

He drew himself forward and hit reply, knowing full well whatever he wrote would go to a phone stolen off some drunk or john, a phone his daughter had used this once then thrown away. He suddenly felt seized by what Ziggy had called the hope that does not exist.

He typed, "I'm sorry and I love you." Stared at the words on the screen. Simple words, easy to type, but which had proven to be too difficult for him to say to his wife when she had been alive and to his daughter before she had run away.

It was moments like these when he felt the full intensity of the drive to drink his brain numb, moments like these when he wanted the courage to dig out the loaded Ruger from the shoebox in his bedroom closet and do more than just stare at it and flip the safety on and off.

He jumped up and turned from the computer. Stumbled. Caught his balance on the back of the recliner and slumped into it.

He sat until the shaking stopped. Then he returned to the chair at the iMac, highlighted the words he had typed, and deleted them.

He swivelled in the chair to face the wall behind the brown leather recliner, and studied the collection of men's faces, painted against dark backgrounds. An artist friend had given them to him. He looked at them, at the weariness he saw in them, at the defeat.

Then he reached for the laptop on the love seat and opened it. Jekyll's instructions about using the Tor browser for navigating to the dark web address in the notebook were simple enough.

It was an underwhelming website, with white Gothic letters on a black background. No dramatic music. No porno sidebars. No moans. No screams. No blood flowing over the page. There was just text informing the searcher that the site was for members only. At the bottom of the page were two rectangular boxes for keying in a username and a password.

Those seeking membership were directed to a second page, where, in order to gain membership, they had to prove with video images that they had a person on hand who they were ready to physically abuse. Once they had obtained membership, their username would rotate through the group. When their name came up, they were expected to go live on the website with a new victim to rape and torture.

Jekyll had printed the username and password of the person who had been uploading from this laptop. The username was *Ant*. The password was *MullMacin*.

Peterson keyed in this username and password and immediately entered a forum for gore and death lovers. The video introduction was a montage of graphic images of war-torn areas: soldiers being shot or blown apart from IEDs, civilians being herded against a wall and executed, bombs blasting in populated areas and bodies flying. Close-ups of mangled bodies, and of faces, some wrenched in pain, others gawking in disbelief. It was the kind of amateur and professional war footage that never made it to the evening or eleven o'clock news.

Jekyll had identified four video uploads from Ant. Fellow members had given this person's submissions five-star ratings, the highest. She also referenced two videos produced and uploaded by another pervert. These had also received five-star ratings.

Peterson clicked on the first of the four videos posted by Ant. The title — *Pandora* — appeared in a Palatino font superimposed on a scenic of the Vancouver skyline with snow-capped mountains in the background. The title dissolved to an exterior of a low-rise apartment building. A woman's muffled voice was begging someone to let her go. Then the camera snap zoomed to a second-floor window, held for a moment, then cut to a bedroom with an unmade bed and peeled yellow wallpaper. A naked woman sat in a chair beside the bed. She raised her bound hands to wipe tears from her terrified thirtysomething face. A male voice, which Peterson recognized as the same voice as in the video of Britney Comer, asked, "What is your name?"

"Angela," the naked woman said.

The interview continued as it had in the Comer video, the voice asking about the woman's past, about her childhood friends. The woman sobbed as she answered the questions.

Then she asked the interviewer, "Why are you doing this?"

Suddenly a man entered the frame. He wore a black-and-white horizontally striped shirt and black sweat pants. He stepped behind Angela and, with great effort, shoved a ball into Angela's mouth and taped it in place.

He looked straight at the camera and said, as though now answering her question, "Ours is not to reason why. Do you know what that means?"

Peterson hit the space bar to pause the video, and studied the thin, frightful looking face. It was almost skeletal, with fiery eyes in dark shadowed sockets. The man had a wispy beard and hair to his shoulders. Peterson was sure this was David Charon.

He hit the space bar and the video resumed playing.

Angela shook her head. Her sweaty brown hair fell over her terrified face.

"No? You don't know what it means?" the man said. "It is a line from a poem about sacrifice. We are all, in one way or another, obligated to sacrifice. It is our duty. There is something beautiful about that. Don't you see it?"

Angela began to cry.

The man leaned close to her left ear and whispered something. Then he grabbed the chair back, tilted it onto its rear legs, and violently threw the chair over onto the floor, Angela with it.

She squirmed to get away from him. Her screams muffled behind the gag.

He removed his sweat pants and dropped to his knees. He said, "If you believe in God, you should pray to Him now."

Peterson cringed at what he saw and flung the laptop onto the love seat. Although he could not see the image on the screen, he could still hear it. Sounds so grimly real they sickened him. He reached for the laptop and shut it off, then left the room to sit on the top step of the back deck. He held his head in his hands.

He sat that way for a few minutes, then lifted his head and looked at his yard, overgrown with more weeds than grass. Paint peeled from the garden shed, and the board and batten door hung on a single hinge. The garden cart stood in high grass in the same place where his wife had left it years ago. The fence needed staining, and two broken cedar fence boards replaced.

He shook his head as if to shake away the thoughts and images that were swirling inside it.

He felt the urge to drink, to go to the glove box in the car and get reacquainted with mister Johnnie Walker. Instead, he walked to the garden shed, pried open the door, and dragged out the Yard Worx lawn mower. From the shed, he retrieved a red gas can that still held an inch or so of gas. He filled the mower's tank, then tried to start it. The mower fired on the fourth pull.

Back and forth, he pushed the mower through the high grass, ripping it as much as cutting. Doing what Dr. Heaney had suggested he do — keep busy when he felt his mind unsettled, get a hobby if he needed to. A hobby, for Christ's sake! He had a hobby, a hobby of sorts, one that didn't lend itself to mental stability. He was mister fix-it.

Back and forth with the mower. Random thinking. Free association of thoughts. Comer and her father. Journalist and backroom politician. Video. Of what? Of who? Comer missing. Rape video. Jesus Christ, what's next?

The mower coughed and sputtered to a stop. Half the lawn was cut. It looked worse than when he had started.

He stowed the mower in the shed. As he returned to the den, the doorbell rang. Three clear tones. He peeked through a glass side panel on the front door and saw the stern face of a female RCMP officer, with her badge and ID held up for him to see.

"Jekyll didn't think you would contact me," she said, after introducing herself as Corporal Collins and following him inside. She had a long face, made to appear longer by her unrelenting frown. "I hope I won't need a warrant to confiscate the laptop."

Peterson led her into the den. "I only watched one of the videos."

"How many are there?" she asked.

"A few."

"We'll watch them together. Take notes if you want. Then I leave with the laptop. Agreed?"

"I don't think I want to see any more," he said.

They sat at the dining room table with the laptop between them. Although he had done so already, he was nervously slow at following Jekyll's instructions for using Tor to re-access the website. Collins took over. Her fingers flew over the keyboard and mouse pad, the way Jekyll's had. In no time, they were watching the same video Peterson had watched an hour ago, Peterson often hanging his head or turning away from the computer screen. When it was over, he had the same sick feeling as before.

Collins saw it and reassured him, "You could've worked a hundred years on the job, Peterson, and you'd never get used to watching this. Child abuse is the worst of it. Live streamed, the same way as this stuff."

Together they watched one rape video after another, and Peterson was thankful Collins was there to watch them with him. The next three had the titles *Hastings*, *Pender*, and *Union*. All had the same format. All shot in ugly, dirty rooms. All ending in the same way, with the camera panning from each victim to a grimy corner of a room, or to an unmade bed, or to a filthy toilet and sink.

After each video there appeared a members' score sheet with star ratings. Each of these videos unanimously received five stars for victim selection and violent content.

"Other gore sites follow a similar procedure," Collins had explained. "Hard to believe, isn't it?"

They watched one of the videos posted by another depraved user. It opened with a fast-paced series of shots of whips, chains, thumbscrews, branding irons, and skull vices, all edited to a melodramatic sound track. What stood out for Collins and Peterson was that intercut with these shots of torture devices were iconic scenes of the city of Halifax: the harbour bridges, Citadel, Public Gardens. The final shot in this montage was of a concrete building in a shabby neighbourhood, and a slow zoom to its basement door. The video they watched was the same one Peterson had seen in Andy Benson's basement torture chamber.

Peterson kept silent about the Benson video, about the phone message from David Charon, and about the link to the video of Britney Comer tied in a chair. He did not want to give up anything to a Mountie he had never worked with before — not until he knew more about what the hell was going on.

He told Collins how he had come by the laptop.

"It was a set-up," he said. "Someone knew I would investigate the files on the hard drive, and get a hacker to open the ones I couldn't."

"Age old question, Peterson."

He looked at her. "I don't know why."

She let it go at that and said, "I think we both have the same bad feeling about this."

Collins left the house with the laptop under her arm. He went and sat on the back deck and stared at the half-mowed lawn. He had made several notes while he and Collins had been viewing the rape videos. Something in each of the videos had struck him as being familiar, something about the rooms in which the rapes had taken place. He pulled out his notebook and reread the notes. His instincts and his thoughts worked together.

He returned to the den, sat at the computer table, and turned on the iMac. He moused over the desktop to the folder in which he stored the email photos his daughter had sent him.

He opened one email after another. It was not until he viewed her emails over the last three months that he saw what had struck him as familiar in the rape videos. A thought suddenly occurred to him. He opened Google maps and typed in an address on East Hastings Street, Vancouver, an address a Vancouver city cop who had once been keeping an eye on Peterson's daughter had sent him a couple of years ago. On the map he read the names of the surrounding streets. Three of them popped out: Pandora, Pender, and Union.

He closed the files and then the folder and turned off the iMac. He stared at the dark screen and felt that what little was left of his life had fallen away to nothing.

CHAPTER
TWENTY-SEVEN

He woke lying on his back on the living room floor. His mouth was parched, his skin clammy, and his head pounded. When he rolled to his side, his stomach went queasy.

On the floor beside him was an empty pint of Johnnie Walker. A near-empty quart of Seagram's was on the oak coffee table. He did not remember going to the liquor store to buy it.

By the angle of sunlight through the kitchen window, he knew it must be mid-morning. He pulled himself to his hands and knees, and got to his feet. Suddenly he remembered the videos and the photos his daughter had emailed to him. After nearly four years, he had cracked the seal on the pint from his glove compartment.

"Oh Christ," he muttered. He felt sick and gagged to hold it down. His breathing quickened and he steadied himself with a hand on a chair back. He stood there for a long time. Teeth clenched. Face stretched. Dry tears.

His cell phone rang and he let it ring. Less than a minute later his landline rang. He went into the den and found the phone on the floor beneath the computer desk. The caller had left a message. Peterson plopped into the brown leather recliner and played it. Hillier had discovered something about Tim Comer and asked Peterson to call him to set up a meeting.

There was an earlier message as well. It had been left on his cell phone at 3:18 a.m., when he had been passed out on the living room floor. It was from an unknown number. He tapped the phone to listen to it.

Thirty seconds of someone breathing, deep-sounding like that of a man. Suddenly a woman let out an unmercifully painful scream, and the line went dead.

Peterson lowered his throbbing head and held it in his hands. Anxious. Trying not to think about the rooms in his daughter's emails matching those in the rape videos. Trying not to think about the possibility of her being in the hands of this madman. Trying not to think of her being something much worse than a victim.

He dragged himself upstairs, where he shivered in a cold shower for nearly ten minutes. Shaved. Gripped the granite-topped vanity and stared at himself in the mirror.

CHAPTER
TWENTY-EIGHT

Hillier joined him on a park bench in a trendy neighbour-hood in the north end. He carried two coffees from Julien's coffee shop across the street and handed one to Peterson.

"You look like you're back drinking," he said.

Peterson laid on a downcast smile and patted his heart. "Mea culpa."

"That means there's not much hope for the rest of us," Hillier said.

Peterson again patted his heart. "Mea maxima culpa." He looked away. Looked back. "Some things are hard to take," he said.

"Understatement," Hillier responded. He carefully loos-ened the tab on the coffee lid, folded it back, and took a sip.

"I have a top-up in the car, if that'll make you feel better," Hillier offered.

"That's the last thing I need." Peterson removed the coffee lid and set it on the bench.

"What set you off?" Hillier asked.

"I'm still putting it together." Peterson said, and winced at what he was thinking.

They drank the coffees and watched a mother and toddler settle onto a bench across from them. She pulled a book from a multi-coloured cloth bag, and read to the child.

"That's a part of my daughter's childhood I missed," Hillier sighed. "Too busy."

"I read to mine," Peterson said. He remembered reading Katy to sleep at night when she was three or four years old. He remembered her reading to him when she entered school. Chicken Little. The Little Red Hen. Thomas the Tank Engine. But never Little Black Sambo. Never that book. It had been off limits, out of bounds. His wife had chosen Katy's books carefully, always on the lookout for political incorrectness. She had been overly protective of their daughter, not just in books, but other things. Play dates. Organized sports. Organized everything. Brownies. Girl Guides. Drive her here. Drive her there. And then her taste of freedom in grade nine, ten. No small bites, not on his daughter's part. She had gobbled.

He drank his coffee. "What about Tim Comer?" he asked.

Hillier continued watching the woman and child. "From the bits and pieces, I think he was pulling a few strings he didn't like pulling," he said.

"The life we bury," Peterson said. At Hillier's puzzled look, he continued, "Something Tim Comer had said. He had stopped enjoying the political power he had, the life he was living, the strings he pulled."

Hillier looked back at the woman and child. "You and Comer were friends?"

"A long time."

"With his wife, too, from what I heard."

Peterson shrugged.

Hillier offered a sneaky smile. "Friends with her more than him?"

"Not really."

Hillier lost the smile. "How often did you and Comer see each other?"

"Not that much, very little in recent years. He was too busy, and I was . . . You know what I was doing. Why?"

"I don't want to blindside you with the little bit I heard."

"Spell it out."

Hillier looked over both shoulders, a man accustomed to trafficking secrets. "A backroom deal that only those high up the food chain knew about," he said.

"High-level source?"

"High enough."

"What kind of deal?"

"Land transfer," Hillier said. Sipped his coffee. "Crown land. Comer's name came up, using his influence."

"A done deal?" Peterson asked.

"No public announcement, but the source said someone's clearing trees."

"Who's the developer?"

"A holding company whose principals are other holding companies whose principals are other holding companies. Mount Everest for all the paperwork."

"Corruption wasn't his style," Peterson insisted.

"Who are you kidding?" Hillier said. "A government deal

177

behind closed doors, that's a backroom boy's world, and you know it."

"I also know what kind of man he was."

"Who would've thought the founding father of our country had been a racist? We all have something. Cradle to grave, there's always something."

A man with a black lab on a leash walked past. He nodded to Hillier and Peterson, and they nodded back.

Hillier got up and went over to pet the dog. Peterson leaned back on the bench and thought about the environmental assessment reports he had seen on Britney Comer's desk and in Tim Comer's office, and about what Bernie had said about Britney's university friend who was a biologist at the Bedford Institute telling about a study that had gone sideways. He also considered Comer's appointment calendar, how her father had avoided meeting with her, and then had finally agreed but had died the day before the meeting.

Hillier returned and sat with his arms folded, sipping his coffee. He looked the solitary man he had become. "There's something else," he said. "Different source. Someone showed a video to Tim Comer, and Comer left the meeting practically in tears. That's what the source said. He wasn't in the room, hearsay, so you can take it for what it's worth."

"Was it associated with the land deal?"

"No idea."

"Who showed it?"

"If the source knew, he wasn't saying."

Peterson walked his and Hillier's empty coffee cups to a trash can ten metres away. He returned to the bench.

"The land deal is probably the political story Britney Comer was working on," Peterson said.

"But I doubt it's the reason she went missing," Hillier said. "That's not a game they play in the backrooms. Don't get me wrong. They're all as crooked as sin. Pressure tactics for sure. But not kidnapping a young woman. I give politicians and the ones making them walk and talk more credit than that. It's someone else, Peterson."

They both got up and walked toward Hillier's Lexus.

"There's a guy doing two years in Burnside for hacking a corporate database," Peterson said. "A nerd. He won't last without protection."

"Are you asking for something else?"

Peterson nodded.

"You're like a leaky faucet."

"I'm sure you know someone."

"I do. But what sugars down on my end?"

"For someone looking to check out early, why do you need anything at all?"

Hillier tried for a hurting face but failed. He shook his head in feigned resignation. Then smiled. "What's the hacker's name?"

CHAPTER
TWENTY-NINE

Barbara Dur showed up ten minutes before their scheduled meeting at the Bluenose Restaurant, two blocks from Number One Government Place. Peterson was already at a table toward the back, out of earshot of the political junkies and newsroom snoops, already into his second dark roast.

She had a face that fit the English equivalent of her French name. Hawkish eyes, steady frown, and a pale complexion that matched her intractable disposition. Feisty was how Tim Comer had once described his secretary to Peterson. But that did not quite capture the scale of her tone and temperament. Rottweiler did.

According to Comer, so did dependable, discreet, devoted, and indispensable. Peterson remembered him saying that she was always at her desk long before 7 a.m., and still there long after the clock-watchers had gone home. Always on top of the ins and outs of current files, and always had policy statements and background reports on his desk long before an upcoming meeting.

There was something else about her that Peterson saw right away. She had even adopted some of Comer's quirky gestures, such as offering her hand with a slight bow, and brushing off the seat and back of a chair before she sat.

"Thank you for coming," Peterson said.

She took the chair opposite him, signalling the approaching waitress that she would not be ordering anything.

Tim Comer would have done that, too, Peterson thought. Appear in a hurry, so as not to slow down an early exit.

"You said it had to do with Mr. Comer's reputation," she said.

She called him "Mr. Comer" and not "Tim," Peterson noted. Gracious, deferential.

"A rumour I want to get to the bottom of, stop it from spreading." Peterson tried sounding nonchalant.

"Why you?" she pressed. Not a shadow of a smile, just the sharp suggestion that an ex-cop who had been forced into early retirement would not have been her first choice.

"Because his wife asked me to."

"His wife? You mean his widow."

She paused ever so slightly before saying the word *widow*, making her insinuation obvious. Old friend offering a widow a shoulder to cry on, doing favours, such as protecting the good name of her husband. That was another thing Comer had said about her. She did her homework on people. Politicians, deputy ministers, lobbyists looking to scratch a few backs. Anyone scheduled to meet with her boss. Detailed evaluations. Including bad habits and indiscretions.

Peterson drank his coffee. "Did you know Tim considered his life in politics a waste?" he said after a moment.

"And you heard that from whom?" Her voice was dismissive.

"Jerry Martin."

"And how credible do you consider Mr. Martin?"

Mister for a street jockey. So polite. "Tim Comer liked him," Peterson said.

"Mr. Comer was a kind man, always sympathetic to lending someone who was down and out a helping hand."

"Monthly meetings, lunch at Chives Restaurant hardly qualifies as a helping hand. They were friends. And what they talked about was what friends talk about. Sports, jobs, wives, life's disappointments."

"I doubt very much Mr. Comer considered his political life a disappointment."

"What if he was pulling strings that ran against his conscience?" He watched her as he said it.

"You cannot be serious."

Not a facial expression to suggest he was on the right track. No tightening in her shoulders. No body movement whatsoever, not a twitch, not even in her hands, which were carefully folded on the table.

An investigator, an old-timer, had once told him to listen to the eyes. The hands, the face, the body language will lie like sin. But the eyes, the eyes are what speak truth.

Peterson asked, "What about Tim pushing a backroom land deal?"

"Not likely," she said.

But her eyes had something different to say. And he held back from allowing a smile to dent his face.

"A parcel of Crown land to a private developer," he continued, making his guess sound like gospel. "Why would he do that?"

"I thought you wanted to preserve Mr. Comer's reputation," she scolded. "But you are making up falsehoods to damage it. I am going to leave, Mr. Peterson, but not before I say this. Timothy Comer was an admirable man, with an ethical standard that was beyond repute. Lies will not tarnish it."

She picked up her purse and stood to go.

Peterson said, "No matter how many ways we twist it around, one and one still make two."

She turned to him.

"Someone was forcing him to do it, blackmailing him with a video," he said.

She bristled and cracked a bitter smile. "I know nothing about a video."

Sure you don't, he thought, but that's not what your eyes are telling me.

He continued, "Tim pressured members of an environmental assessment committee to favour the transaction," he said, making it up on the fly, using the report he had seen in Britney Comer's office and what Bernie had said about a biologist at the Bedford Institute.

"He would never do that."

"Not unless someone was forcing him to. Was Tim the subject of the video? Compromised in some way?"

"He was not."

Peterson leaned forward. "Not compromised, or not in the video?"

She looked confused.

"I don't want to destroy Tim Comer's reputation," he said. "We were friends most of our lives. I respected him as much as you do, maybe more."

Barbara Dur tilted her head to one side and threw him a contemptuous look.

"If you respected him," she said indignantly, "then you would be more judicious in the words you chose."

"Who was in the video?" he pressed.

Her face hardened, but her eyes dimmed with sorrow and discontent.

"Was his daughter onto the land deal?"

Without another word, Barbara Dur turned from him, and left.

He watched her walk past the front window. Stoic. Loyal. He sat thinking for a long time, then pulled his black notebook, opened it, and read a few pages. He turned to a blank page and wrote: *Video — Not political. Personal.*

The server, college age and pretty, came over to top up his coffee. He saw her coming and placed a hand over his mug. She moved on to serve a couple at a nearby table.

He returned to the notebook, underlined the word *Personal*, then drew a large question mark beside it.

CHAPTER
THIRTY

An hour later he cruised the side streets, following Jerry Martin's usual route. There was no sign of Martin and his grocery cart. The crew at the bottle exchange hadn't seen him in days. That worried Peterson. One of them, a twenty-something with tats around his neck like a necklace of barbed wire said Martin had been banned from cashing his bottles and cans there. He had blown up at the manager for something, threatened him with a broken bottle.

Peterson walked among the crates and bins to a raised, glassed-in office. Overseeing the operation was a tall man, midforties, with cropped blond hair and a nickel-plated smile. He stood as Peterson entered the office and offered his hand. Introduced himself as Farley Barnstead. When Peterson asked about Jerry Martin, Barnstead raised his right hand for Peterson to stop right there.

"I have nothing to say about him," Barnstead said.

"Martin and I go back a lot of years," Peterson said. "I know he has problems, but I can't help him if I don't know what happened."

Barnstead thought about it, then relented. "He came in to cash in a cartload of bottles, and just snapped."

"Snapped?"

"Blew his top over nothing. Only I know it's never over nothing. I'm a vet too. One tour in Afghanistan was more than enough. I never saw what Martin saw, but I know other vets who saw a lot of bad shit go down. Only with Martin it's been getting worse and worse. Blaming people."

"For what?"

"For everything. I don't know. He just started screaming about what someone did."

"Who?"

"No name, just someone, you know, pointing his finger at nothing and screaming."

"Was he screaming like that when he broke a bottle and threatened you?"

Barnstead gave an acquiescent shrug. "It scared the hell out of me. I was backed up between two bins and had nowhere to run. You get scared like that, your mind goes crazy until the training kicks in. Stood my ground. Then whatever was driving him nuts went away. He backed out and threw the bottle in the street."

Peterson thanked him, and Barnstead shrugged.

"I'd hate to see what happens if somebody cuts him off," he said.

"What do you mean?"

"Blocks his way. Traps him in."

• • •

The building super answered Peterson's buzz on the intercom. Peterson explained who he was and that Jerry Martin was a friend who was going through a bad stretch.

The super came to the front door to let him in.

"A bad stretch doesn't cut it," the super said. He was short, chubby, and growing forehead. "The owner wants him evicted. He wrecked the place. I'll show you."

The stairway to the second floor held a sinus-clearing smell of industrial cleaner and body fluids. The super was used to it. Peterson breathed through his mouth.

The super's comment that Martin had wrecked the apartment bordered on understatement. In the living room, what little furniture there was had been thrown about. Holes decorated all four walls. Beneath one large hole, lying on the laminate floor, was a smashed thumb drive.

In the bathroom the toilet seat had been ripped off. The mirror over a small pressboard vanity was smashed, and glass filled the sink bowl.

A window had been broken in the kitchen. Fridge toppled. One of two ladder-back pine chairs had been turned upside down, and the bottom rails crushed. Brown cupboard doors were open, and the contents emptied onto the floor. A pale green landline had been yanked from the wall and flung across the room.

"He was all right most of the time," the super was saying. "Talked to himself a lot, but who doesn't do that?"

Peterson asked if he could look around, and the super told him to fill his boots. He left, saying if Peterson needed anything else, he was in apartment number one.

After the super had gone, Peterson went from room to room, unsure what he was looking for. In the kitchen, on the side of the cupboard beside where the phone had hung, names and phone numbers had been written on the wall. One of them, number only, was twice as large as the others. He recognized it as Tim Comer's office number. In smaller printing beneath it was what Peterson guessed to be Comer's cell number. He pulled his iPhone and punched it in. After several rings, it went to message. Tim Comer's voice said he was unavailable. Peterson hung up.

Across the kitchen, lying open in a corner where it must have been flung, he saw a telephone directory. It had a grimy cover with a photo of Peggy's Cove. A slew of phone numbers had been written on the cover. One of them stood out by having been circled several times. Peterson pulled out his iPhone and opened the Safari browser. He entered the 411.ca website address, clicked on reverse search, and keyed in the number off Martin's phone book cover. It was for a real estate development company located on the Bedford Highway, the Benson Group.

Next, he googled the company name, then double clicked the link to the Benson Group's website. The project page featured various developments from high-rise office towers, apartment buildings, and residential housing. Another page showed artist sketches of a projected seaside resort: a three-storey hotel complex, restaurants, a café, cottages, tennis courts, an eighteen-hole golf course, and a marina. There was also a page for the company's executives. First up was the President and CEO, Toby Benson. Late thirties, tanned face, square jaw, teeth-whitened smile, deep brown eyes, and wavy salt-and-pepper hair.

Next to the President and CEO was a photo of Andrew Benson, Vice President and Project Manager. Shaved head. Riveting blue eyes. Peterson guessed his title was an empty one, more pomp than actual responsibility. Though Andy Benson was listed as four years younger than Toby, he had a thin, deeply lined old man's face. A heavy duty drug user, was Peterson's immediate impression.

He looked back over the room. Something struck him. He knelt, picked up the smashed thumb drive, and shoved it into his jacket pocket.

After making another circuit of the kitchen, bedroom, and living room, he closed the door behind him, making sure the lock clicked, descended the stairway, and cop-knocked on the super's door.

"Did Martin get many visitors?"

The super laughed. "A woman," he said. "Lena something or other. Scrawny like she hadn't eaten in a month. She had those eyes that pop out. I talked to her once, and I couldn't stop looking at them."

"Any idea where I can find her?"

"Yeah, I see her around, mostly at the McDonald's on Quinpool. A few times I've seen Martin with her. There's a section on one side, and she usually sits to the back of it."

Peterson started to go, but the super stopped him.

"You said you know him."

"I do."

"Like for how many years?"

"Since we were kids," Peterson said.

"Then tell me something. He has an army disability pension, and from what I heard his girlfriend has an army pension too. So how come they live like that, you know, collecting bottles, bumming from cars stopped at traffic lights."

"I don't know," Peterson said. "Why does anyone live the way they do?"

CHAPTER
THIRTY-ONE

At the information desk in the Summer Street lobby, he asked for the room number of Dr. Heaney. The receptionist behind the desk searched the patient list and replied that there was no patient of that name. Peterson realized at once what Danny Little had done. He had admitted Dr. Heaney under a different name to protect the victim and possible witness from further attack.

Peterson stepped away from the information desk and called Bernie. She answered on the first ring.

"I'm at the hospital. Where's Danny hiding her?"

"He knew you would ask," Bernie said.

His impatience showed in his voice as he told her how much he owed that old woman — his life, if that was worth anything.

"He's lead investigator," Bernie appealed.

"And you owe him what?"

There was a short silence as she thought about it. Then she released a long and loud sigh. "We admitted her under the name Rita Beazley."

Peterson negotiated his way past the nurses' station and along a hallway cluttered with scales, a gurney, two used linen bins, a padded armchair on wheels, three IV poles, and a rolling cabinet stuffed with towels, sheets, and johnny shirts. There was no security on the door — too much of a giveaway — and the semi-private room also helped maintain the cover.

Dr. Heaney had the window bed, overlooking an urban farm. Her roommate was not there, likely off for tests or some medical procedure. A male housekeeper haphazardly ran a cleaning cloth over bedrails, bed trays, chair arms, and cushions. No attention to detail. No interest. Peterson waited for him to leave.

Heaney sensed Peterson standing in the doorway. She looked up from her book and smiled as broadly as her black-and-blue face would allow.

"So much for police security," she wheezed, still smiling. "But I should have known you'd be the one to breach it."

He pulled up a chair beside her bed. Took inventory of the deep purple bruises on her face, neck, and arms, of her shaved head and the three-inch laceration with multiple black stitches. Her short, wincing breaths suggested body bruising and probably one or more broken ribs.

He asked the usual questions for a hospital visit, and she answered with half-hearted remarks about bed comfort, institutional food, the never-ending pokes from blood techs, and the inconvenient sleep interruptions for the taking of vitals. Then she asked about him and watched his hazel eyes lose their gleam and his smile morph into a frown.

"Nothing changes overnight," he said.

And she responded. "But after months of counselling."

"I'm still hiding from myself."

"But you're not without hope."

"That's a four-letter word," he said, trying to match the faint smile wincing over her face.

"Your mother didn't think so when she named you God's Love, or its Greek equivalent."

His lips puckered with sentiment. "I haven't been called that since before my mother died."

"It doesn't quite describe the man you became, but it does offer some insight into her expectations. Life plays tricks on us, Peterson. It lines the road with obstacles. Some are more difficult than others to climb over. We never sought to bury the circumstances of your life, but to reconcile them with the torment inside your head. You are not a bad man, Peterson. Very few are."

He looked at her. "What about the man who did this to you?" he pressed. "Was he bad?"

"I don't know him," she said. "I only know what he did. The difference being, I know the violent things you have done, whether you intended to do them or not. But I have also come to know something more about you. You don't just do for yourself. There is meaning in what you do, a purpose. And behind it is a desire to do something good."

He sank into the chair and drifted his eyes past Heaney and out the window. He told her about Britney Comer, the video link David Charon had sent him, about Charon's wild raving, and that he was certain his daughter was involved with him.

He turned to her. "Did you see your attacker?"

"I know why you're asking," she said. "And I'd prefer the police handle it."

"Shoulder length black hair," he prodded. "Eyes that see right through you."

She turned away from him and closed her eyes. "Don't pile hurt on top of hurt. For your sake, please don't."

"He got into your computer and copied the recording from our last session," he said.

"I know." She opened her eyes and looked at him. "He laughed about it. He said he was going to kill you."

● ● ●

Peterson went back to the information desk and asked the receptionist for the room number of Mrs. Stokes. The receptionist directed him to the Dickson Centre in the Victoria building down the street. The Dickson Centre treated cancer patients.

He walked the three blocks and stopped at the main-floor gift shop in the Victoria building. Looked around, but did not see anything he could bring to a woman who was dying of cancer. In the elevator, he stared at his feet and listened to a man with a ball cap on backward tell a woman, in the voice of a know-it-all, that the doctor and nurse had it wrong about what they were telling the woman about her brother.

Along the 9B hallway, Peterson flinched at the smell, as though dying people had a stink all their own. Patients walked by, stood in doorways, or lay in beds with their eyes fixed on nothing. Sunken faces. Walking skeletons pushing IV poles. He stopped at a door and looked in.

Benny Stokes sat in a straight-back chair beside the bed on the window side of the room. His wife lay with her eyes closed, her grey-streaked brown hair sprayed over the pillow. Stokes looked up, saw Peterson, and came to the door.

Peterson said, "I came by to see how she's doing."

"Not too good," Stokes said. "Come on in. Meet her."

Reluctantly, Peterson followed Stokes to the bedside. Stokes repositioned the bed table so Peterson could get close. At the head of the bed, there was an IV drip from a bag of clear liquid. Stokes's wife opened her grey, spiritless eyes.

"Sandy, this is Peterson. I told you about him. He came by to say hello."

Sandy smiled through the painkillers.

Peterson smiled back, the uncomfortable smile of someone not knowing what to say. Then he said what he felt, "I'm sorry you're dying. I'm sorry it can't be easier."

She looked at Stokes then back at Peterson. "I'm scared," she said. Her words were somewhat slurred. "I never died before."

Peterson's eyes widened as he coughed out a grunt, as though a fist had slammed into his chest. He lowered into the chair Stokes had been sitting on, and reached out and touched Sandy's arm.

"I'm scared too," he said. "We all are. We just hide it pretty good."

Her face had the look of crying, but there were no tears.

"I can't hide it no more," she said.

Stokes reached down and rubbed her leg. He started to say something, but Sandy shook her head for him not to. She quietly lay there, staring at the ceiling, breathing as though she needed to catch her breath.

Peterson still had his hand on her left arm.

She groaned, but her faint smile suggested it was not from pain. She took a few deep breaths, then said, "Benny talks about there being something else. Do you believe there is?"

Peterson squeezed her arm and shook his head. "No. I don't believe in it."

She reached her right hand across her body and rested it on his hand. She made the same crying face. "I don't think it would make it easier."

He rotated his hand to hold hers. He held it for a long time.

• • •

Stokes walked him to the bank of elevators. Nothing said. When the elevator doors opened, Stokes started to cry. "I love her," he said.

"That's why it hurts so much," Peterson said. "That's the deal."

• • •

Roger Stiles met him in the cafeteria of East Hants Rural High School. Tall, thin, shaggy dark hair, face droopy and shadowed in a midforties gloom. His handshake came with the breathy smell of tarred rope.

Stiles had worked computer forensics until the federal government, on a cost-saving move, had closed the East Coast lab and redirected most forensic analysis to Montreal and Ottawa. The best Stiles could come up with on such short notice, if he wanted to stay in his wife's home province, was teaching computer programming in a rural high school. As it turned out — and as Peterson knew from a chance meeting a year before in a north end coffee shop — teaching provided Stiles with a satisfaction his forensics career had not.

Stiles led Peterson from the cafeteria and down a long hallway to the computer resource centre, where Stiles had a small computer repair niche behind a blue room divider at the back. They sat at a maple-topped work table and caught up on the past twelve months, Stiles a lot more forthcoming than Peterson. Then Peterson withdrew the thumb drive from his pocket and asked if it was salvageable.

Stiles looked the thumb drive over.

"Someone had a good go at it," he said. "Stomped on it more than once. How important?"

"Not sure if it's important at all."

"Curious enough to go a bottle of ten-year-old Talisker single malt?"

"I can do that," Peterson agreed.

"No splitsies," Stiles called.

Peterson chuckled. "How hard is it to repair?"

"It won't be easy."

"How long?"

"If I get the drive to work, there's no guarantee the data will be intact."

"How long?"

"How long is a string?" Stiles smiled.

● ● ●

Peterson had just crossed the McKay Bridge when his phone vibrated with a text message: "THIS ONE'S FOR YOU." There was also a link to a Tor website. He didn't click the link — not yet.

An accident on the bridge side of the Robie Street exit had backed up traffic. An ambulance, fire truck, and two police cars were on the scene. More stop than go. Time to think.

He pulled pen and notebook. After drawing a series of boxes, he filled them with words and names: *Land Deal*, *Holding Company*, *Tim Comer*, *Britney Comer*, *Assessments*. Beside the word *Assessments* he scratched a question mark. He had started connecting the boxes when the traffic moved forward.

Once off the exit ramp, he swung up a side street, and shortcut his way to The Office. "I need to use your computer," he said to Cotter, who was behind the bar pulling drafts and loading them onto a tray for Janice to deliver.

"You need a hell of a lot more than that," Cotter replied. He slid to the end of the bar where Peterson was standing. Lowered his voice. "Look at you." He pointed to the mirror behind the bar. "Open book."

Peterson did not look.

"I don't want to hear about it," Cotter said, his low voice scolding. "You go all this time without a drink. Jesus Christ!" His head jerked side to side.

Peterson went stone-faced, much the way he had done when he was ten years old, standing on that grassy slope with his father outside the psychiatric hospital, looking up at his mother in a third-floor window in a white hospital gown, waving to him, and him refusing to wave back.

At the opposite end of the bar, a man with a cucumber face called for a beer.

Cotter raised an index finger to signal that he would be right there. He turned back to Peterson. "No matter how hard it gets, you can't lower your guard."

Peterson started to say something, but Cotter stopped him.

"Not for an instant," Cotter said, "or the urge will grab you by the throat."

He went down the bar to pull cucumber-face a draft. As he reached for the yellow wooden tap handle, he paused to gesture to his upstairs flat and said to Peterson, "You know where it is."

● ● ●

In Cotter's office the Tor address brought Peterson to a site with a red play button on a yellow background. The button almost filled the screen. Words slowly crawled across the frame above it: "Hell Is Hopeless." Username and password required.

He keyed in the username and password Jekyll had given him — *Ant* and *MullMacin* — and hit the play button. The button dissolved to video of a couple lying in bed in a room he remembered seeing in one of the rape videos. The date, 29 September, was superimposed at the bottom of the frame. That was almost three weeks ago.

One of the people was his daughter, her lacklustre

brown hair sprayed on a pillow, dull eyes, scowling face. One of her breasts was unashamedly exposed. On her side of the bed was a cardboard box standing on end, and on the box was a foil-wrapped cube and a glass crack pipe with black burn marks on the outside.

The other person was a man not much older than his daughter, with long hair, also propped on a pillow, covers pulled aside, naked. Snake tats on his arms. The man was David Charon.

"And what else?" Charon said.

His daughter shrugged, mumbling what sounded like "I don't know."

"It doesn't sound like the worst thing you can do," Charon said.

They lay in silence for a while, both staring at the ceiling, and then he said, "I killed people. Liked it, you know. Raping them and watching them die. Uploads and scoring big."

"Huh?"

"Someone wants to pay me to do it again. Online bud."

She turned to him. Gave a loopy smile.

"Like with the kittens, three of them, three little kittens," he said.

"Huh?"

"With the kittens."

"Lost their mittens," she said. Giggled. Reached for the crack pipe. "The doll house," she said. The blanket slipped and exposed her other breast.

"Not good enough," he said. He looked at her. "I wanted to see them inside. That's what I should've done. Put a camera inside. Upload them burning."

She shook her head. "They were kittens."

"Be better with people," he said, taking the crack pipe from her and reaching across her to replace it on the cardboard box. "A camera inside watching. Like God watching, you know, big head up in the sky like the Wizard of Oz. Upload it, that's what I'll do. I'm seeing it happen inside my head. Hearing them, people I mean, screaming. Five-star."

He went back to staring at the ceiling.

Peterson watched. Aghast. His daughter, naked, bleary eyed, stoned. And he was listening to her, to them. The craziness of what Charon was saying. And his daughter. Her voice sluggish, going along for the blow, or smack, or whatever the hell would keep her high.

"That's what someone wants me to do," Charon said. "That's why I'm here, why I'm fucking you. Keep you high. Bring you with me to torture your old man. Payback for a friend back home."

"Huh?"

"A cop."

"My father was a cop."

"Yeah, a bad cop."

"Bad father."

"Deserves what I give him."

Katy raised a hand and stared at it, as though seeing her hand for the first time, intrigued.

Charon continued to stare at the ceiling. "You never answered me," he said.

"Answer what?"

"The worst thing."

She dropped her hand to her chest. "I don't know."

"You can help," he said. "Like you did with those women.

Bringing them here. You can help like that. Only worse. Sweet, huh. Five-star."

Her eyes widened. "What?"

"That's what someone wants." He rolled to his side to face her, his back to camera. Cruelty in his voice. "Old friend of yours. Your father too. How bad is that, huh." He rolled to his back. Smiling. Dreamy eyed. "That's sweet. That's fucking five-star." He angled his head toward her and started laughing.

The video ended.

Peterson stared at the black screen, burdened with a hopeless yearning for something — anything — other than what he had seen on that screen.

• • •

Wave after wave crested a hundred or so metres from shore, then rolled to the cobble beach. The backwash was a staccato of castanets. Wave after wave. Continuous, as though there were no before and no after. His wife and daughter had called this beach their beach. For two summers in a row, they would come during the supper hour, the three of them, to walk, or sit, or dance with the waves, or simply watch them crest and tumble. And often, while his wife and daughter played along the beach, he would stare out to sea. He was staring out to sea now, searching for an illusion that could help him live with what he now knew about his daughter. What he saw instead frightened him.

He dropped to his knees and punched at the cobbles, with each punch crying out "Christ Almighty, Christ Almighty," until his knuckles bled.

He returned to his car. His hands swollen. They could barely grip the steering wheel.

"No," he cried out, as he fought back the desperate craving to disappear into the darkness of an everlasting drunk.

CHAPTER
THIRTY-TWO

Flashing red, blue, and white lights. A dozen or so cars crawled along the coastal road as the drivers slowed past the three police cruisers blocking the parking area to the Herring Cove look-off. Peterson's beat-up Chevy was one of them.

Upon seeing Bernie's red Honda Civic parked alongside the cruisers, steering with the palms of his hands, he pulled to the opposite side of the road and sat there for a while composing himself. A dozen or so cars passed before he got out and crossed to where the forensics van, rear doors open, had angled near a footpath that led down through scrub spruce to the water's edge, to where Britney Comer's clothes had been found. Bernie stood beside the van. She saw him and waved to one of the uniformed cops to let him pass.

They walked to the cliff edge, to where a dozen huge boulders had been set to prevent vehicles from driving over.

A strong wind rolled up whitecaps. Bernie tugged down the bill of her blue ball cap. Looking out to sea.

He faced the same direction, looking down to the spume off the waves breaking over a large flat rock.

"We have a body, or what looks like one," she said. "Two arms, two legs, a head, and a torso. Missing left middle finger. The body was laid out like it was intact. Bled out somewhere else. Between the fingers of the right hand was a health card. Stephanie Gail Zola."

He ran his swollen hand over his head.

"I hope you didn't bruise those knuckles on someone's face," she said.

"A beach I didn't care for," he grumbled, looking out at the whitecaps.

"Was it something the beach said, or something it did?"

He watched a couple of container ships waiting in the offing for tugs and the pilot boat to conduct them to one of the terminals in the harbour.

"Zola was helping Comer with a story about prostitution," he said.

"Yeah, I know. Comer's boyfriend told me that. How come you didn't? I thought we agreed to share and share alike. What am I supposed to think?"

He continued looking out to sea. He said, "Zola and Comer got into a blue SUV, a Ford Explorer. Neither had been seen since." He looked down to where the forensics team was bagging the dismembered body.

"Source?" she asked.

"A prostitute named Buffy, and Zola's half-brother, Leechy Murphy"

"That jerk wouldn't tell me anything," she said.

"He needed persuading."

"I'll bet he did."

A forensics tech called out to Bernie, saying Danny wanted her down below.

"What aren't you telling me, Peterson?"

He pressed his hands together under his chin, as though in prayer.

Bernie's face flushed. "I'll be expecting you at the station at three this afternoon, ready to talk. Otherwise I'll have a warrant for your arrest for obstructing a police investigation."

He shrugged and shoved his hands into his pants pockets. "Make it tomorrow. No, better yet, the day after. I have a few things to do yet."

Her voice seethed. "It was a woman's body, for Christ's sake!"

Into the silence that followed he said, "We both know damn well that detective work has nothing to do with figuring anything out. It's all about milking your sources."

"And you're a detective again."

"Unpaid."

"What sources are we talking about?"

He shook his head and looked out over the water. "I need time to know who the parasites are," he said.

"And telling me something now compromises that?"

He didn't answer.

"Who are you protecting?"

He ignored that question too. "Two days," he said.

She glared at him. "Twenty-four hours, or we'll lock you up."

CHAPTER
THIRTY-THREE

Stiles phoned and told Peterson he had repaired the thumb drive, but the data had been corrupted. It contained a four-and-a-half-minute Motion JPEG file, an iMovie, of which he had managed to recover four frames from various parts of the file.

After forty-five minutes of busting ass along the coastal road, through the city, and out the 101 to East Hants Rural High, Peterson had to sit on a hard wooden bench in the hallway outside the vice principal's office and wait for Stiles's class to end. A scowling teenage boy sat on the bench next to him. Now and again the kid glanced at Peterson, but mostly he studied the floor at his feet

"What'd you do?" Peterson asked.

The kid ignored him.

Peterson turned his attention to the open door to the secretary's office, where a young woman, early twenties, with flyaway brown hair sat at a desktop computer with her head turned to look over her right shoulder. She was staring at him.

After a couple of minutes of this, she got up and came from the office and stood before him.

"You don't remember me," she said. "But I remember you. I was working in a gas bar. You saved my life."

Peterson looked away out of embarrassment. He saw the teenage boy looking at him with a face full of curiosity. He turned back to the woman, shrugged, and shook his head.

"Thank you," she said, knowing full well that he remembered.

And he did. Eight years ago he had been returning to the city from Hantsport after interviewing a possible witness about a drug hit in the city. Running on fumes. His headlights swept a highway sign indicating gas off the next exit. Half a click and he made the combo six-pump gas bar and convenience store, which was flooded with hard fluorescent light.

Two cars were unattended at the pumps: a blue minivan with a child's car seat, and a black Firebird with the engine running, heavy bass on the stereo. Spinners. A teenager with short hair worked inside behind the counter. A man in a brown bomber jacket and red ball cap cocked to one side stood five feet away with his arms hanging stiff at his sides.

Peterson climbed from the Jetta and filled the tank. Angled his body sideways to the convenience store, facing the dark country road. Sneaking a glance to the plate glass window. A car drove by and kept going. The gauge hit fifty bucks and he stopped pumping. He racked the nozzle, closed the gas cover, and circled to the driver's side. He opened the door and leaned in, reaching down under the driver's seat for a twelve-inch nail puller. He slid it up the sleeve of his forest green jacket and cupped the claw with his hand.

He blew into the convenience store, all smiles. The teen, a seventeen- or eighteen-year-old girl, was still frozen in place behind the counter, wide eyes blinking non-stop. The guy in the bomber jacket hadn't moved either.

Peterson glanced up at the convex security mirror in the far corner and saw a young woman huddled over her baby at the dairy case in the back of the store. He also saw the guy in the bomber jacket hiding the .38 behind his leg.

"Pump number three," he said to the teen behind the counter. He had no sooner said it than he was in motion. Dropping the nail puller from his sleeve and into his hand. Dancing a pirouette as he raised his arm faster than bomber-jacket could raise his. He chopped down and felt bone break. The .38 dropped to the floor.

He came up hard with the nail puller into bomber-jacket's groin. Doubling him over. Then he slid his hand up the iron and racked it upward to catch the guy across the nose. He kicked the handgun out of reach as the guy hit the floor, face bloody.

He walked to the back of the store and crouched down to the woman and child. Her long brown hair hid her face the way her body covered her child.

On the floor beside them was a red plastic shopping basket that contained a bag of chips, bagged milk, and a box of melting Popsicles.

"It's over," he whispered, and showed her his badge. "You're safe, and it's all over."

She raised her head to look at him. He nodded and smiled, her face broke into pieces, and the cry she had choked in her throat for the last so many minutes chuckled out like water from a narrow-necked bottle.

He was still remembering, still lost to that moment, oblivious to the secretary thanking him again and returning to her desk, unconscious of the teenager getting up and entering the vice principal's office. It required Stiles tapping his shoulder to awaken him to where he was and why.

Two minutes later he and Stiles were back in the computer resource centre, with the repaired flash drive running off Stiles's MacBook Pro. The image on the screen was of a woman in a hotel lobby, shot by a ceiling-mounted security camera. Even blown up, her face was unrecognizable.

"Mean anything?" Stiles asked.

"Not yet."

Stiles played the video. They watched thirty seconds of diagonal black scratches across an image of orange and green. At a flash frame, Stiles hit the space bar to stop the video. He backed up one frame at a time. He stopped at a distorted image of what appeared to be the same woman opening a door.

Stiles now advanced the video forty-two frames to an image of a closed door bearing the number 427.

Seeing it took Peterson by surprise. He stiffened and folded his hands under his chin.

Stiles noted his reaction. "Important?"

"It could be. What else is there?"

Stiles advanced more than a hundred frames, to the next image of a woman's left hand, with diamond ring and wedding band, in the process of cutting out a line of coke with a razor blade.

"That's it," Stiles said. "Make any sense?"

Peterson continued staring at the hand on the screen.

"This is what I miss the most," Stiles said. "The bits and pieces. Seeing if they tell a story."

CHAPTER
THIRTY-FOUR

Raylene O'Connell was waiting for him at the front door, a bit unsteady as she leaned forward to kiss his cheek. No smell of booze.

"You look terrible," she said. "Have you started again?"

He flinched, but did not answer.

"Why?"

He looked ashamed. "Things happened," he said.

"Like what?"

He shrugged it off and gestured that they should enter the house. He followed her to a flagstone patio that overlooked the mouth of the harbour. She wore Jesus Jeans and a bulky grey sweater. Her brown hair hung loose to her shoulders. They sat in brightly coloured armchairs at a table fashioned from a millstone and set on a pedestal of cut granite. There was a sterling silver Thermos and two dark blue pottery coffee mugs on the table.

She had been working on a mug of coffee.

"Can I pour you one?" she asked, and reached for the Thermos. Thought better of it and asked him to pour his own.

"I'm trying," she said. "But I don't know how to get through this. I know we weren't close, but I'm her mother. I'm supposed to . . . For God's sake, what am I supposed to feel when my daughter is missing? Of course I'm worried. Who wouldn't be? I mean what . . . ? There are no instructions, no manual. But there are phone calls. Sympathetic voices offering advice, gloating, as though I'm the one. Not the victim, but . . . As though I deserve it. They don't call me a bitch, but that's what they're saying, the tone they use. Sticky sweet."

He finished pouring himself a mug of coffee.

"I need to go back to work," she said, "but I can't, not like this. I can't be seen like this."

He sipped his coffee and watched her face shape itself to her thoughts, from perplexed to distracted, from disturbed to aggrieved.

"The police are no further than the last time they called," she complained. "What are they doing?" She locked eyes with him. Her voice lowered, and her tone was berating. "What are you doing?"

He buckled down the urge to tell her that Britney had climbed into a blue SUV outside the Horseshoe Tavern, and that a crazy named David Charon had texted him a video link that showed Britney tied in a chair, and that this morning the police had found Stephanie Zola's chopped-up body in the same place where Britney's clothes had been found. Instead he asked, "What was Tim working on before his heart attack?"

"What?"

"Before he died, what was he working on?"

"You mean specifically?"

"That's what I mean."

She was peeved. "I don't know, specifically. It could've been anything from party policy to helping draft legislation."

"He didn't talk about it?"

"There was a lot in government he didn't talk about."

"What about a land deal?"

"A land deal?"

"The transfer of Crown land?"

"Why would something like that involve him?" Now she sounded offended.

"I heard about a meeting he had," he said. "I think Britney found out about it." He was being vague on purpose, and watching her eyes as she connected the dots.

"A meeting with who?"

"With someone about a land deal."

"I still don't understand."

"Tim was into something."

"Something? Someone? Why are you doing this?" she pleaded. "The questions, the way you're asking them."

"I'm just asking about the transfer of Crown land."

"But why?"

He studied her face, worked the silence a moment longer.

"The premier and cabinet listened to him," he said. "They took his advice. Most of the time it worked out, but sometimes . . ."

"He wasn't God, Peterson. He made mistakes." She brought her hands from her lap and ran one through her hair.

"I suppose," he said, "but this one was different."

"Different?"

He saw the confusion in her eyes. Her apprehension. He sipped the coffee, then set down the empty mug.

"The transfer of Crown land is no big deal, not usually," he confided. "Sometimes it's just a land swap of some kind. A private developer gives the government a piece of land in exchange for one owned by the Crown. A simple exchange, but only after the government does an environmental impact study. That's where a deal can get delayed, or refused. I think the land deal Tim was brokering didn't pass the test. But it went ahead anyway."

She looked off into space, pretending what he had said was not part of her life. Then she swallowed dryly, and looked at him.

"He helped set up the nature conservancy," she protested. "Tim would never—"

"Not unless he was forced to."

Her shoulders straightened, eyes narrowed. "Do you know how much influence he had, how much power?"

Peterson let her reprimand settle over him. He never took his eyes off of hers. He calmly said, "Maybe someone had more power than him. Maybe that person had something that stripped Tim of whatever power he had. It could be anything, you know. It could be a video of someone in a hotel room doing something she shouldn't be doing."

And there it was, the shameful recognition. She grunted

as though struck solidly in the guts. Her shoulders dipped. Her eyes filled.

"The night I got you out of that hotel room," he said, "I busted in. Too much of a hurry. Faces didn't register. I remember you were sitting on the edge of the bed crying, and there was a guy doing a line at a desk with his back to me. He never turned around. And there was someone else with the covers pulled over his head."

O'Connell's face went mushy.

He leaned across the granite table to take her hands and hold them tight. He looked down at her engagement ring and wedding band. "Booze and white powder, Ray, they've been your weakness for a long time. Who was supplying you?"

She would not look at him. Her voice was contrite. "It was a fundraiser for the children's hospital. We went back to his room. I didn't know they were recording it."

"Whose room, Ray?"

She shook her head.

"Should I make a wild guess based on what little I know?"

She still would not look at him.

"I'd say it was someone interested in a backroom land deal," he said. "Someone whose younger brother has an inside track to a coke supply, who's been supplying you for years. Someone who fancied himself a filmmaker. Britney and my daughter had been running his errands. That's how Britney found out about you. I didn't know it then, but that's why she came to me. She wanted me to put Benson behind bars. Only six months wasn't enough, and he was back with your regular supply of nose candy. Am I close?"

O'Connell pulled her hands away and nearly knocked the mug to the flagstone floor. She pushed it aside and laced her hands on the table. Unlaced them. Re-gripped the mug.

"With coke on the table, it wasn't hard for him to get you into that hotel room," he said. "iPhone video. A star is born."

"I had no idea," she appealed.

"Andy Benson had to be the one with the camera. I'm pretty sure of that. And Toby was too smart to be there. So who was the other man?"

She turned her body away from him and faced the ocean view.

"I doubt a coke-using wife would have been enough to blackmail Tim Comer into doing what he would've been dead set against doing. And I doubt you blowing dope and going two-on-one with Andy Benson and just any man would have driven him over the top. It had to be someone important. So who was it, Ray? Who was the other man?"

She spoke to the waves cresting over a rocky shoal. "It never happened again, never."

"Don't say that," he railed. "Not to me. Not when I know too much. Just tell me who?"

She pulled at her hair, and without facing him, she said, "It wasn't a man."

That stunned him. It took him a moment to gather himself.

"A woman? A prostitute?"

She shook her head.

"Who was it?" he demanded.

His voice had her shaking. She let go of her hair and stared at him. "Please."

"Tell me."

"Leanne Bobbitt."

"Bobbitt?"

For the second time within the last minute or so, she had taken him unawares. She meant the woman who had been in the first video he'd watched, the one who'd gone missing a year before.

"Jesus Christ, I . . ." he said.

O'Connell stiffened and sat upright. "Don't go there, Peterson. Don't think it."

"Benson was taking pictures of you and Bobbitt in bed together," he charged.

"I didn't know he was."

"Then I bust in and get you out, and who knows what the hell happened after that."

"But I wasn't there," she shouted. "You know I wasn't there!"

"What the hell good is that? Accessory before the fact. Who knows what else."

He turned away from her, holding his fists chest high and shaking them. Then he faced her. "No wonder Tim buckled under blackmail."

She cowed under his sharp eyes.

"A friend of Britney's told her about the environmental report going against the land deal," he said. "Tim used his influence. Britney's not dumb. She wanted to ask Tim about it. I think she was also asking a lot of questions, probably to the wrong people. Tell me how Tim died."

"You know how he died." Her voice was biting.

"I know what his obituary said."

"Then read the death certificate."

He saw the corners of her mouth fall and her body shrink inside itself. He pressed, "Which room was it?"

She did not answer.

"In his office? In here?"

She did not answer.

"Your husband with a bad heart on the floor or slumped in a chair. You finding him. Making a 911 call. Ambulance, police responding. I can read the report, if there is one."

She glared at him, and her hands shook. The empty coffee mug knocked against the millstone. She turned away from him. Then she suddenly turned back. "He had a massive coronary," she snapped.

He calmly leaned forward and reached out and folded both her hands between his, settling them. He listened to the fear he saw in her eyes.

"There was no call to 911," he said. His tone was so matter of fact, making his deduction so convincing, so like a detective with a suspect in the box, stuffing down his own feelings to get at whatever came close to being the truth. "No police. No paramedics. And no report. But there was a death certificate."

She pulled her hands from his and got up. Using the table and a chair for support, she walked to a fieldstone wall, beyond which the ground sloped sharply to a footpath twenty metres below.

"You don't think I know what a family doctor might do for a friend?" he said. "So I'll ask again. How did Tim die?"

She took her time, drawing deep breaths to steady herself. She pointed to the footpath below and told him to follow it. Then she made her way, unsteadily, up to the house.

The path was a switch back down to the water, through a stand of poplar and white birch. Halfway down, beneath an old white birch, which was at least twenty inches at the butt, there was a cedar garden bench fastened to a slab of concrete. The bench had been angled to provide an ocean view through a cleared section in the trees. Tim's and Ray's names had been wood-burned into the back of the bench. On the seat was a blue and yellow porcelain vase, and in it was a dozen freshly cut red roses. Peterson lifted his eyes to a limb that hung out over the bench. He saw where a narrow section of the bark had been chaffed away.

He returned to the house. She was sitting in one of the swivel chairs and staring out the window. She held a highball glass, and as he entered, she drained it.

"I'm not going back to work," she conceded. "Not for a while."

He remained standing. "Andy Benson was into violent porn. Uploads to the web. He could have uploaded the video of you. I'll do what I can. No promises." Then his voice filled with a sense of being injured. "Did Tim leave you a note?"

He watched her body shiver and her face contort into a painful expression. She shook her head, stood, and pressed herself against him. "Please, Peterson."

He turned from her and left the house.

CHAPTER
THIRTY-FIVE

He found Martin's girlfriend Lena Jay sitting in the Quinpool Road McDonald's, where the super had said she always sat. Working on an extra large Coke, a caffeine substitute for the small "c" her pasty face and skin-and-bones body indicated she hungered for. The lifeless, scraggly hair that hung to her shoulders had that crack user's look, and it reminded him of what he had seen on his daughter in the last video.

As he crammed his solid frame into the blue resin chair across the table from her, and without looking at him, she said, "You're Peterson."

He nodded. She added, "Jerry said sooner or later you'd show up."

"Where is he?"

She sipped the Coke. "I don't think he wants anyone to know."

"Not even you?"

She looked at him, and in that dispirited gaze he saw a world of hurt and disappointment.

"He told me about it," she said. "He figured it out."

"From the thumb drive Comer had given him?"

Her smile was like a mouthful of lemon. "Two women going at it. Nothing new in that. Until Jerry told me one of them was Comer's wife."

A half-hearted smile creased Peterson's lips. "Did he tell you about the other woman?"

She stuck out her lower lip. Peterson took that as a no.

"Her name was Leanne Bobbitt," he said. "She ended up dead."

"Jerry never said that," Lena said, and stared at Peterson. "He did what Comer wanted him to do. Comer couldn't face going to Benson himself. Jerry went for him. They were good friends, him and Jerry."

"Did Jerry think smashing the thumb drive would end it? Is that what Toby Benson told him, that there were no other copies? What guarantee did he get?"

She responded as though she hadn't heard or understood what he had said. "I never seen two men bonded so tight."

Her attention went to several high school teens entering the side section of McDonald's and sitting at the front window overlooking the street. Talking loud. Scooching around.

"The thumb drive," he reminded her. "Did Benson tell Jerry that's all there was?"

She offered no response.

He waited. He patiently waited as she watched the teens. Her expression swung between interest and anger.

Finally she turned to him. "I know about thumb drives," she growled. "So does Jerry and so did Comer. Toby Benson guaranteed he'd erase the original. Jerry thought it was bullshit."

"Where is he?" Peterson pushed.

She shrugged. "Like I said." She sipped the Coke and over the brim locked eyes with him. "Fifteen-year age difference. I think he's more fucked up than me."

"What makes you think that?" he said to keep her talking.

Her straw slurped the bottom of the empty cup. She frowned and said, "I don't want to talk no more."

He dug a card from his wallet and handed it to her. "If he calls."

CHAPTER
THIRTY-SIX

Peterson sat on the folding chair beside the desk with the iMacs interconnected and watched Jekyll play the keyboard and mouse. As blurred swimmings of numbers, letters, and keyboard symbols flashed across the screens, she grunted, groaned, and sometimes sighed with disappointment.

She had smiled when she met him at the front door, and thanked him for the protection he had arranged for her friend. Now she was more than willing to do another hacking job for him. But not until he had told her what it was all about. As much as she was beholden to him, she did not want a hack job that would land her in the same situation as her friend.

He had told her about the video being used to blackmail Tim Comer, a highly influential backroom strategist, into manipulating a change in an environmental assessment report then advising the premier and two cabinet ministers to make a secret deal that transferred Crown land to a private developer. She had asked if this had to do with the last hack job she had done for him. He had double clutched on that one. Finally he had said, "It's like two paths alongside each other, and I'm never sure which one I'm walking down."

A half hour passed, an hour. Peterson had already made a coffee run to a nearby Tim Hortons, and now he was on his feet ready to go for another black coffee for himself and a latte for her.

"I'm in," she cried, expressing the hacker's rush of getting into a corporation's database by uncharacteristically beaming and flinging her arms above her head in the touchdown salute. Then, catching herself, she dropped her arms to gesture to the monitors with both hands.

"In?" He pulled the folding chair closer to hers.

"His personal and corporate accounts are on the same server," she said, still buoyant from her successful hack job. "We can look at what ever we want. Financial statements. Internal memos."

"Just the video," he cautioned.

She shrugged down her excitement and went to work. With a couple of keyboard clicks, she brought up the photo file. She played the mouse to scan through a slew of PR shots, the usual boilerplate photos for media distribution, mostly of Toby Benson and political dignitaries breaking ground at various locations, architectural drawings and computer-generated models of building projects, business meetings, staff photos.

There were separate files for senior staff. She double-clicked the one for Toby Benson, and moused through hundreds of photos and videos of Benson at his desk,

Benson conferring with colleagues and some identifiable politicians, Benson in white hard hat at dozens of construction sites, sitting in a bulldozer, a backhoe, on his hands and knees laying sod.

"What about personal?" Peterson asked.

"Not a problem. His devices are all synced, and everything's backed up to the corporate hard drives. All of his personal photos and videos should be here."

Jekyll had already downloaded an arts association photo of Raylene O'Connell, and another of O'Connell chairing a board meeting for the Tourism Industry Association of Nova Scotia. She ran proprietary facial recognition software, which came with her work for the RCMP.

It produced one hit, a video that was on a backup hard drive.

"We're lucky it was online," she said, and started playing the video.

The video opened with a montage of shots of the Marriott hotel edited to the painful squeal of heavy metal guitar.

Jeykll groaned at the sound of it.

The last shot in the montage was of the hotel seen from across the harbour. This shot lap-dissolved to the hotel's front entrance. A woman entered from left of frame and walked into the hotel. Peterson recognized her.

"That's enough," he said. "That's the video."

Jekyll played the keyboard and deleted the video.

Next, Jeykll accessed the Internet. Using the same software, she conducted a thorough online search for photos and video of Raylene O'Connell. Other than several media shots of her at an arts gala, participating with government officials at the opening of new tourist information centres, and a few innocuous Facebook uploads by friends and family, there was nothing online that compromised Raylene. And in Peterson's mind, there was nothing connecting her to the death of Leanne Bobbitt.

"Now what?" Jeykll asked.

He smiled sadly. "I have to talk to a friend then keep a hot date with a good looking cop."

CHAPTER
THIRTY-SEVEN

Peterson and Hillier got out of Hillier's silver Lexus and walked toward the seawall in Fleming Park on the Northwest Arm, the long finger of water that defined the west side of the Halifax peninsula.

"He's dropping bread crumbs," Hillier said.

Peterson agreed.

"No brainer then," Hillier concluded. "You need help doing this."

They reached the seawall of cut granite blocks and stopped for a moment to watch the sailboats from yacht clubs further out on the Arm raising sail. Sunlight popped off the coloured canvas and gleamed in the spume cutting off the bows of boats running clean with the wind.

"She's your daughter," Hillier said. "It's about nothing else but protecting her."

They started up the seawall toward the harbour mouth.

"They'll jail her," Peterson said.

"Safer place for her. And a good lawyer could shorten her stay," Hillier said.

"I tried that with the daughter of a friend, Joe Christmas," Peterson said. "She came out a mental wreck. Katy would go through the same hell."

"What about the hell she's going through now? I saw enough of that video to know she's being used by a god-damn lunatic."

Peterson's face lengthened like unbaked dough. His mouth went through two stages of hurt.

They reached a section of seawall where granite blocks encased a two-metre-diameter pool, which was used as a catch basin for hillside runoff. Hillier sat on one of these blocks and retied his left shoe.

"How many times did we both make excuses for not getting them the kind of help they needed?" he said. "Our daughters crawled in and out of our lives, drugged up and pissing themselves, desperate, and we looked the other way."

"Doing time was not what they needed," Peterson said with regret.

"And drugs fucking up their lives was?" Hillier said with scorn. Then his voice lowered. "I can't look back without it hurting so much. The mistake I made . . . you . . ."

Peterson cut him off and walked past a boat ramp to where an old man in a beat-up Expos cap was fishing off a dock. "How many?" he asked.

The old man looked into the white plastic twenty-litre bucket at his feet. "Two."

"Two what?"

"Cod," the old man said, and lifted a fourteen-incher from the bucket for Peterson to see.

He and Hillier walked on, past the Dingle Tower, a four-sided ten-storey structure overlooking the Arm, past a play-ground with a wooden replica of the Tower. An anxious mother stood with her arms positioned to catch her four-year-old, who was climbing a rope ladder. There were other caregivers — mothers, grandmothers, a dad — pushing kids on swings, guiding them down slides, pumping the handle on a water pump and filling a water bottle.

"You don't even know where she is," Hillier challenged.

"He said something about coming home," Peterson said. "Nail that location down and I . . ."

"You what? Go in armed to the teeth, with your daughter in there with him? What happens if . . . ?"

"What happens if I don't?"

"He doesn't care who he kills, Peterson. You heard him. He wants to kill in front of a camera and upload it. He kills for the fun of it. He's the worst kind."

"That's why I can't leave her there."

"But you can't do it on your own."

Peterson was not buying it, and he knew his face showed his irritation.

They walked in silence to where the seawall ended and a narrow footpath began. It continued along the west side of the Arm, behind enormous multi-roof single-family houses, with rolling lawns and sculpted hedges. Some had boathouses and wharfs with various sized sailboats moored beside them.

Peterson stopped and looked from one side of the Arm to the other. Grunted a scornful laugh. "A lot of wealth out here," he said.

"Most is legit, some not so much," Hillier added.

"You should know about the not so much," Peterson said.

"Yeah I should, but my house wasn't on the water. Same neighbourhood, one block up. I wasn't running with the big dogs."

"Andy Benson one of those big dogs?"

Hillier sharpened his stare. "You got the key in the right hands. That's when you're supposed to let it go."

"Just asking."

"You're never just asking, Peterson."

"Did you ever defend Toby Benson?"

"He flew lower than his brother. But there was once, domestic violence. He beat up a girlfriend so bad . . . short fuse, but his kind always do. Big shot. Can't take no for an answer. What's with you and him?"

Peterson pointed across the water to a white house that was larger than most others, oriented at an angle on the lot so the rear and side wall had spectacular views of the harbour mouth. Both walls were practically all glass.

"There's another home owner who shouldn't throw stones," Peterson said.

Hillier looked at the white house. He looked at Peterson. "What's going on?"

"Something I can't do anything about," Peterson grumbled.

"I don't understand."

Peterson shrugged. "Toby Benson was blackmailing Tim Comer on that land deal. No evidence, and even if there was, I wouldn't use it."

"The video," Hillier guessed.

Peterson nodded.

"Comer's wife," Hillier guessed.

Peterson did not answer.

They retraced their steps along the footpath to the sea-wall. Hillier looked as though he was arguing with himself. After walking a ways, Hillier held up his hand. He had something to say, and by the firmness of his stance and the determined look he gave, he had made up his mind to say it.

"The stinking holes we crawl in and out of," Hillier said. His eyes were sad and gloomy. "What if I could help?"

"Not if that means going with me."

Hillier nodded reluctantly.

"It won't be a courtroom we'll be walking into," Peterson warned.

"I know."

"You don't know, Hillier. Believe me, you don't know."

"I know I need to do something."

Peterson shook him off, slowly, firmly.

Hillier frowned, then chuckled. "I'm suicidal, for Christ's sake. What the hell difference does it make where it comes from?"

CHAPTER
THIRTY-EIGHT

Bernie met him at reception and led him, as though he didn't know the way, through the investigation unit, a honeycomb of back-to-back desks separated by grey room dividers.

"You still have two hours to spare," she teased.

"I didn't want you jumping the gun."

"Danny was keen, and I had a warrant ready."

They reached the workspace Peterson had once shared with Danny Little. Bernie's side of the back-to-back was a lot neater than he had ever kept it. He could hear Danny now. All those years together, and every day it was the same complaint: "How can you find anything in this mess."

"Danny booked the broom closet," Bernie said, grabbing a file off the desk. "He's waiting on us."

"He doesn't want to be seen walking the halls with me," Peterson said.

She rolled her eyes.

The broom closet was a small meeting room detectives used to escape the hustle of the investigation unit; some to think through a file, some for a one-on-one with another detective, and a few — Peterson had been one of them — to sleep off a weekend or weeknight drunk.

Danny sat at a table with its maple-laminated top lifting at the edges. With his head down as Peterson entered, he pretended to be writing something on a yellow legal-sized pad.

There were four chairs around the table, and at one of them was a desktop computer.

Bernie took a chair beside the computer and across from Danny.

Peterson remained standing. He had been eager to get this done, but Danny's cold shoulder now slowed him down. Peterson deliberately tore a page from his notebook and placed it on the keyboard of the computer. It contained Jekyll's instructions for the Tor browser and accessing the rape videos on the .onion websites. Passwords included. He then set his iPhone on the table and slowly slid it, as though unwilling to give it up, to Bernie. He had been careful to erase the video link in Charon's text message, showing Charon and Katy in bed and Charon talking about killing Britney Comer and him. From his hip pocket he withdrew the blue Birks jewellery box and placed it on the table nearest Danny.

"Start with the video message on the phone," Peterson said. "That was texted to me the other night, followed by a phone call from a crazy man named David Charon, ranting about the story of Little Black Sambo and God being a metaphor." Bernie gave a questioning look. He added, "Don't ask until you watch all the videos. The web addresses and passwords are on the paper. Take your time. I'll be in the coffee room." He smiled to Bernie. "I know the way."

• • •

Jamie Gould had been holding down the coffee room since he had made detective. He worked his investigations from there. Peterson could see that by the files spread out on the white Formica table — the guy always had liked it in there. Crossword on the go. So long as he produced results, the brass left him alone. So did most of the other detectives, including his partner. Gould looked up as Peterson entered, went to the coffee machine, and pulled a mug of coffee.

"What brings you here?" Gould asked.

Peterson leaned back against the counter. "A few questions about the file on Britney Comer."

"I heard you knew her. What are you doing, helping Danny the Dickhead with the investigation?"

Peterson coughed on a sip of coffee.

Gould laughed. "It's like he suddenly forgot where he came from. Don't get me wrong. I like Danny Little. He came with a cred, like you. But since you went out on your ass, he's walking around like someone pulled his foreskin over his head. And to think the two of you were tight. So seriously, are you helping on that file?"

"Not really. Something just came my way and I brought it in," Peterson said.

"Like the key to a warehouse in the Battlefield." Gould smiled. "Jackpot."

"Yeah?"

"Don't give me that," Gould said. "You know goddamn well what was inside that basement. Andy Benson's going up on everything from sexual abuse, assault with intent, forced confinement of Leanne Bobbitt, and if forensics finds her DNA in the bloodstains on the floor or in the drain pipe, we'll be charging him with murder."

"I smell promotion."

"Let me tell you, it beats the hell out everything else I've been working on. Best distraction from the home front I ever had."

"How so?"

"Trouble with my parents," Gould complained. He sounded like a teenager. "Six months ago my old man turned sixty-two and gave himself a birthday present — early retirement. My mother's head was spinning. She couldn't figure out what she was going to do with him around all the time. Then a month after he retires, she came home from grocery shopping with an idea for their fortieth anniversary. He told her he had an idea of his own, started packing suitcases, and loaded them into his car. She wasn't part of his idea."

"Another woman?"

"Who knows? He hasn't surfaced yet. He left a lawyer to manage the sale of the house and assets. I figure when it all sugars down, she'll move in with me. Other than that, I'm living the life, you know, eating more, drinking more, more of everything except what I sometimes go home to get." The grin returned to Gould's face.

Peterson went at his coffee.

"You didn't come down here just for a visit," Gould said.

"I need a favour."

"After what you did for me? Anything. But what's the matter, too shy to ask Bernie?"

"I'm keeping her out of it. The Dickhead too," Peterson said.

Again Gould flashed a big grin.

Peterson pulled out his notebook. "I'm looking for David Charon. He grew up in Nova Scotia. I want to know where he lived."

"Does this have anything to do with Benson?"

"They're both crazy, if that's a connection."

"How long ago did Charon live here?"

"I'm guessing under five years, could be longer." Peterson pressed a finger to his lips.

"Understood," Gould nodded.

Bernie stepped into the doorway and leaned against the jamb, as though she needed it for support.

"We've seen more than enough," she said to Peterson.

He shoved off the counter and, as he followed her from the room, turned back to Gould and held his fist to his ear to signal Gould to call him.

At the broom closet, Bernie stopped and asked, "What is Gould doing for you?"

"Tracking down a good-looking woman I once saw passing by," he said.

"That's misuse of a police database," she cautioned.

"And you never ran a tracer on a guy you met," he kidded.

"You're a bad liar, Peterson." She folded her arms. Jaw set. He knew she would hound him until he fed her something she could swallow.

"My daughter," he said.

"What about her?"

"I heard she was in town, and Gould works the gutter."

"It's nice to know you don't think I work it too."

"Homicide comes with status."

"I'm glad you think so."

"No respect?"

"Not the professional kind," Bernie grumbled.

"The Harrison case still a fiasco with Fultz screwing up the crime scene?"

Bernie grunted a laugh then said, "Tell me about your daughter."

"What's to tell that you haven't already heard?"

"She could have changed, Peterson. Give her the benefit."

"I'm hoping so," he said, and let it go at that.

Danny sat with his eyes closed. Bernie took the same chair across from him. Again Peterson remained standing, favouring Bernie's side of the table.

Danny opened the jewellery box.

"Emerald green fingernail polish," he said. "Pretty good match for the dismembered body we found on the beach."

"Stephanie Zola," Peterson said.

"And it just turned up in your mailbox," Bernie said.

"Close," Peterson said. "Ziggy Glover was a guarantee to pass it on to me."

"Who gave it to him?" Danny asked, still staring at it.

"A guy named David Charon."

"Claim to fame?"

"The crazy man who sent me the text and phone messages," Peterson said. "He's the one who picked up Comer and Stephanie Zola outside the Horseshoe Tavern."

"Why did Charon want Glover to give it to you?" Danny asked, looking at Peterson for the first time.

"To get me involved."

"And why is that?" Danny demanded.

Peterson had already calculated how much to tell and how much to hold tight — enough to make them happy, even put them on the scent, but not enough for them to get out ahead of him. He said, "It has to do with my daughter." He turned to Bernie, making it obvious he was playing her as the lead detective. "He knew my daughter in Vancouver. Britney Comer had been her best friend. I think he's getting even for something they did a few years ago."

"Getting even with your daughter, or with you?" Bernie asked.

Peterson sensed she had tweaked on to something. He covered his face and drew his hands down to cup his jaw. Playing the role. "I don't know. I think Charon's doing it for someone else." He pulled a strained look. How convincing it was he could not tell. "The thing is I don't know how it comes together. Not yet."

Bernie was about to ask another question, but Danny bolted forward. Finger pointing.

"This is our investigation," he asserted. "I'm telling you to back off right now."

Peterson glared at him and calmly said, "The way you should back off the Harrison investigation."

Danny shot daggers at Bernie.

Peterson continued, "We covered for one another, Dan. But not if it meant back-stabbing another cop."

"Stand down," Danny scowled, "or I do what I wanted to do before you came here."

Peterson extended his arms in a gesture for Danny to cuff him.

"Put your arms down," Bernie said. Calmly taking charge. "Now what about those rape videos?"

"Yeah, what about them?" Danny demanded, still trying to stare Peterson down.

"Charon has been following me for days, probably weeks," he said, addressing Bernie, again making it obvious he considered her the showrunner. "He knew I hung out at The Office, and it would not have taken him long to link me to Janice Doyle, who waits tables there. He came on to Janice's sister, Ellen Doyle, they played a little, then he beat her up, knowing she'd tell her sister and her sister would tell me. He left a laptop at Doyle's house, which got me to the porn sites and, with the help of a hacker, to the sites on the dark web."

"And of course you looked at them," Bernie said.

Peterson raised his hands in surrender. "I'm a detective."

"Was a detective," Danny growled, and rapped his knuckles on the tabletop.

Peterson gave him a ready smile. "That makes two of us."

Danny balled his hands into fists, then slowly set them on the table. "What's with you and Comer's mother?"

"She asked me to help find her daughter."

"Why you?" Danny pressed.

It was the same question Barbara Dur had asked him, and with the same demeaning intonation.

"You know as well as anyone that me, O'Connell, and Tim Comer grew up together. We maintained a friendship over the years."

"What was she suspicious of?" Bernie asked.

He sensed her eyes searching his face and reading his body language. And he knew if he overplayed it, she would see it. So he played it straight, saying, "She wanted to know before you did about her daughter's disappearance."

"Maybe find out if the daughter was into something the mother wasn't," Little sneered. "We know all about her." He placed an index finger beside his nose in a coke snorting gesture. "So what was she doing, getting you to stop blow-back on her and her husband's good names?"

Peterson repeated a line from Hillier, "Don't ask, don't know, don't have to tell." He looked at Danny Little and lowered his voice to enhance the meaning in his words. "Maybe she was a friend whose friendship I took seriously. Maybe I wasn't willing to leave a friend out to dry."

Little swelled like a plugged volcano. His fingers gripped the edge of the tabletop and tightened.

Bernie must have seen Little was about to blow. She rotated in the chair to face Peterson squarely. "Do you think Comer's disappearance has anything to do with her father? Big shot in government. Was there dirt we should know about?"

"No," Peterson said.

"Sure about that?" Bernie asked, saying it as though she knew more than she was letting on.

"Not sure, no." Peterson backpedalled.

"So the father had a little dirt," Bernie emphasized.

"What politician doesn't?"

"Cagey answer," Bernie said.

"There was a document, a report of some kind," Peterson responded, throwing her a bone. "Norton at CTV told me that."

"She told you and not us," Danny pounced, slamming his left hand on the table. "You're not a cop, why the hell would she tell you anything?"

Peterson's face lit up. "The Peterson charm."

It was like holding out red meat to a hungry dog.

"You rat's ass," Danny flared. "You have something on her."

"That's part of the charm, Dan."

"I could charge her for withholding evidence."

"Good luck with making that stick to a journalist."

"You know what the problem is here . . ." Danny began.

"Let him finish," Bernie cut in, clearly annoyed. "What about the document?"

"Norton never saw it. I never saw it." He leaned over the table, resting both hands on it. "But I think you should go back and talk to that biologist friend of Comer's. He gave her something to get her asking questions about an altered environmental assessment report."

"Which involved her father," Bernie said.

"She had scheduled a meeting with him," Peterson said. "Maybe it was to talk about what she knew. Check with his secretary, Barbara Dur. The meeting never came off. He died the day before. Coronary."

Little and Bernie exchanged looks. A technique Peterson had often used to make a suspect think he had given something away. Peterson let it ride.

"Are we done?" he asked.

"No, we're not done," Little commanded.

Peterson stared at him. Waited.

Embarrassed that he had no further questions, Little

went back to making notes on the legal pad. Without looking up he muttered, "Get the hell out of here."

● ● ●

As Peterson snapped on his seatbelt and cranked the engine, coaxing it with a little more gas, Bernie opened the passenger side door and got in.

"Oscar winning performance," she said, picking up an empty coffee cup at her feet and placing it in a drink holder in the centre console. "Needle Danny to keep him off balance. Then tell us what we wanted to hear. But not all of it. You kept some to yourself, and I think it was the most important bits, like what your daughter's role is in all of this. And don't say you're still working it out. I have a son, and I would say anything and do anything to protect him."

Peterson stared straight ahead. He did not answer.

"Should I make a guess?"

He checked for traffic in the side mirror, then shifted into gear.

"We going somewhere?" she said.

"I am. You can ride along if you want." He pulled out and drove to the traffic light at Cunard Street.

"She's helping this David Charon, isn't she?"

He kept his eyes on the road so she couldn't see the truth in them.

"How?"

The light changed, and he hung a left and headed for the Halifax Commons, a wide-open urban park with ball fields, a cricket pitch, and a speed-skating oval, which at this time of year accommodated roller blades and skateboards. At North Park Street, he negotiated the roundabout and struck out north on Agricola Street, then wove his way through side streets, avoiding traffic, and driving into a Lawtons drug store parking lot. He stopped, shifted into park, then circled his arms around the steering wheel, and, still without looking her way, said, "I can sit here as long as you."

Bernie laughed lightly. She opened the door and said, "I'll hitch a ride back."

Just then his cell rang. He didn't recognize the caller ID but answered it anyway. It was Jerry Martin's girlfriend, Lena Jay. Her voice stressed.

"Jerry was just here," she screamed. "I don't know what the fuck's going on."

"Calm down, Lena," Peterson said in a voice evenly modulated. "Take a deep breath. Okay, now tell me."

Bernie got back into the car.

"Army Navy store," Lena whimpered.

"What?"

"He bought camouflage. He's wearing it."

"Where's he going?"

"I don't fucking know!"

"What did he say?"

"Nothing. He just went wild. Throwing things. Showed me a combat knife, Mark 3. He said he'll cut her up."

CHAPTER
THIRTY-NINE

Tearing across the intersections and shortcutting through parking lots. Squealing tires. Bernie asking. Him not answering. Not about Raylene O'Connell. Not about Jerry Martin. And not about Tim Comer dying, hanging himself. What he did answer was that Jerry Martin was out to get even with a knife.

"Why?"

Peterson spun the wheel onto Purcells Cove Road. Tapped the brakes in a hairpin turn, then gunned it past the Greek church, the Armdale Yacht Club, through a four-way stop, and out toward the cliffside homes.

Bernie pulled out her cell and tapped a text message.

"Martin called her a bitch of a woman," Peterson said.

"Why?"

Peterson dodged a FedEx truck, ducking the question. Flew past the turn for a Parks Canada fort and then past the Herring Cove look-off. Pedal to the floor. The shitbox Chevy giving him what he was asking for. One-thirty in an eighty-click zone. Bernie on her phone to Danny Little. Then ordering Peterson to slow down. Him boosting the speed. Passing a black Camry on a double line and just missing an oncoming taxi returning to the city.

"We find nothing, and I'll write you up," she threatened.

"You know we'll find something," he answered.

Roadside birch and spruce a blur. School bus flashing yellow. Taking it before it went red. Then ripping into the Storm View driveway and through the open front gate. Tunnel of red maple. Gaping front door.

They got out, and Bernie unsnapped the safety catch on her waistband holster.

"You better be right," she said as they slipped through the front door and into the living room with the captain's chairs facing the glass wall and ocean view.

They speed-scanned the room. Seeing no one, they separated to sidle along opposite walls. As Peterson climbed the three steps to Tim Comer's office, Bernie turned down a hallway toward the bedrooms.

In the office, he saw the glass-topped kidney-shaped desk had been smashed and the MacBook Pro flung across the room at the bank of windows with the coastal view. He returned to the living room, then proceeded through an informal, open-concept dining room where photographs had been removed from an interior wall, smashed, and tossed into a pile beneath a double-hung window. There must have been a dozen photos. Two stood out. One was a wedding photo of Tim and Raylene standing on a stone bridge across a small stream in the Halifax Public Gardens. The other was of four teenagers standing on a dock, a Cape Island boat tied up beside it. The teens had their arms around one another's shoulders, the boys bare-chested and the girl in a one-piece. From left to right, the teens were Peterson, Tim Comer, Raylene O'Connell, and Jerry Martin. All were smiling like they hadn't a care in the world.

Bernie was waiting for him in the living room. She shook her head, and he shook his. Then he chinned toward the door that led out to the flagstone patio.

One of the brightly coloured chairs had been knocked over, and there was an empty highball glass on the millstone table. Peterson gestured for Bernie to follow him, and he led the way to the path that switchbacked down to the water. After passing through the stand of poplar and white birch, they rounded a turn and saw Jerry Martin standing on the seat of the cedar garden bench. He had a knife in his right hand. O'Connell was balancing on the back of the bench with support from Martin's left hand. Her hands were tied behind her back, and there was a rope around her neck.

"Christ," Bernie said.

When Martin saw Bernie and Peterson rounding the turn, he raised the knife to O'Connell's stomach and shouted for them to stop.

They stopped close enough to see O'Connell's trembling jaw and frightened eyes. Bernie stepped to one side of the path, angled her body, and widened her stance. She inched her right hand toward the holstered Glock.

Martin saw the move she had made and shouted. "Draw it out with your little finger, or I gut this bitch."

Bernie did as ordered, hooking the trigger guard with her pinky, lifting the Glock from the holster, and dropping it to the ground.

From up near the house Peterson heard a car door slam shut. He opened his arms in supplication. "This won't go where you want it to go," he said.

Martin angrily shook his head. "Goes where it goes." He pressed the knife to O'Connell's belly, and she squealed and flinched away and almost lost her balance.

"No, Jerry," Peterson begged. He lowered his voice. "Protecting her is protecting Tim. Sure, we know how she was. But he always forgave her. The things she did and the hurt he went through."

"With you," Martin scoffed.

"When we were kids. You too. You had as much a crush. You joined up because of her, to get away."

"It was fucked up."

"But this won't make it right," Peterson acknowledged.

"Yes it will," Martin yelled.

Bernie took a small step closer to the cedar bench.

"It won't bring him back," Peterson said. "For Christ's sake, Jerry, you hang her and it's like hanging Tim twice. We both know how much he loved her."

Martin grimaced. He pointed the knife at Peterson and growled. "And look what she did to him."

"It wasn't her that drove him to it," Peterson said. "It was Toby Benson blackmailing Tim over a development deal."

"Toby Benson's dead," Martin said, his knife hand lowering slightly.

Peterson's shoulders sank. He sighed. "Oh, Jerry, what the hell did you do?" He raised his shaking hands and cradled his head. He was scared, the way he had been scared in the container terminal, knowing the drug dealer would have ridden their standoff to the very end. Knowing that by killing Benson, Martin was now doing the same thing. He had no way out.

Bernie inched forward. Peterson did, too, reading Martin's eyes, looking for a chance to make a move.

From behind them, Danny shouted, "Drop the knife. Drop the fucking knife."

Martin's head jerked upward. He saw Danny. Then he scowled at Peterson and screamed at the top of his lungs. He cocked his right shoulder and drove the knife into Raylene's stomach and thrust it upward.

The force launched her off the cedar bench, and the noose tightened. Blood spurted as Martin pulled out the knife.

Peterson lunged to grab and hold up Raylene's bloody body.

Bernie jumped at Martin. He swung and slashed her across the right cheek. She howled and fell to the ground. He re-gripped the knife for a stabbing stroke and advanced toward her.

Peterson turned to Danny and hollered, "Shoot! Shoot!"

Danny just stood there with his right arm extended and the pistol aimed at Martin. Eyes wide. Teeth clenched. Groaning in his struggle to pull the trigger.

Martin reached Bernie, dropped to his knees, and raised the knife over his head.

"Shoot!"

Danny fired. Three shots. Centre mass.

The impact flung Martin backward and four feet down the path.

Quickly Danny was on him. He grabbed the knife off the ground and cut the rope tied to the trunk of the yellow birch.

Peterson lowered Raylene to the bench. Her blouse and jeans were soaked in blood. So much blood spurting up his arms as he pressed his hands against her stomach to stop the bleeding. He pulled off his coat and pressed it against the spurting blood.

"Help me," he cried.

Danny tried to help, pressing his hands over Peterson's. But the knife had plunged deep, and the upward thrust had stabbed under her breastbone and into her heart.

CHAPTER
FORTY

When the police and paramedics arrived, Danny was standing over Martin's body, staring at it. A uniformed cop picked up the Glock at Danny's feet, turned him away from the body, and guided him up the path.

Peterson was sitting on the ground beside O'Connell's body, which was still sprawled on the cedar bench. His clothes, hands, and face were soaked in blood. His eyes were glassy, and he was shaking uncontrollably. A paramedic wrapped a grey blanket around him, knelt, and started asking him questions, which he did not understand.

Another uniformed cop came over, and he and the paramedic helped Peterson to his feet and led him up the path to where flashing red, blue, and white lights had transformed Storm View into a macabre carnival of colour.

Peterson's Chevy and Danny Little's white Malibu had been pushed onto the grass on one side of the circular driveway to make way for an ambulance and two police cars. Another ambulance and two more blue-and-whites had parked along the driveway in the tunnel of red maple. Still another cop car was parked on the roadside, and one of the cops was directing traffic.

Through the open rear door of one of the ambulances, Peterson saw a paramedic tending the knife slash along Bernie's cheek. Then, sitting her in a jump seat and buckling her in. Closing the door.

Danny sat in the shotgun seat of a police car, and when the cop and paramedic ducked Peterson into the back, Little continued staring straight ahead. His late-middle-aged face had hardened into the look of a deep-lined sixty-year-old. When Peterson asked him how he was doing, Danny started to weep.

• • •

Jamie Gould met them in the emergency room. Eyes popping. Hair a mess.

"They're stitching her face now," he said, and held up thumb and index finger. "Missed losing her eye by this much. Are you all right?" He looked at Peterson, then at Little.

The two of them nodded. Stunned.

Inside a curtained cubicle, Peterson removed his bloody clothes and pulled on blue scrubs, which an ER nurse had handed him after she confirmed with Gould they would be returned. Fifteen minutes with an ER doc and Peterson was cleared to go. Danny too. Gould drove them to the station, where uniformed cops had delivered Danny's Malibu and Peterson's Chevy. Gould wanted separate statements about what had happened at Storm View. Danny went first.

Peterson had kept his statement tight at first, then, realizing there was no one left to protect, told Gould the details about how Raylene O'Connell, Leanne Bobbitt, and Andy Benson had engaged in a drug-fuelled night of sex in the Marriott hotel; about Andy Benson recording that night; and about his brother, Toby, using the video to blackmail Tim Comer. He also told Gould that Jerry Martin's revenge on O'Connell and Toby Benson was for having driven Comer to hang himself.

When Peterson finished and signed his statement, Gould held up a slip of paper. "It's a good thing my name's down on the debit side of your ledger, because otherwise I shouldn't give you this." Gould handed Peterson the slip of paper.

"David Charon was sixteen when his parents died," Gould said. "Murder–suicide. The mother had been shot dead with a Lee-Enfield .303. The father popped himself with an old .45 revolver. That's the address where he grew up. Social service records are vague about where he lived after his parents died, but he graduated from the high school he had been going to, so he must've continued living in the area." He flashed a curious smile and continued. "The Mounties are investigating the sicko videos you passed them. I'm guessing they belonged to this Charon."

Peterson nodded.

"Did you know that Charon and Andy Benson shared a hell of a lot more than just being loony tunes? They were both uploading to the same site on the dark web."

Peterson nodded, as though he had expected as much.

"We got a warrant for Benson's email account and hard drives," Gould continued. "He had gore and porn videos up the ying yang. Downloaded some, but most were ones he made. A lot of violence, a lot of slime. I went back six months on his emails. Three months ago a name popped up. David Charon. They go back and forth about liking each other's videos, the ones they upload to the gore site on the dark web. Seemed like a regular competition. Bragging rights on being the most violent. Anyway, they soon figured out they're from the same province. One still living there, the other on the west coast. Up until a few days ago, when I brought Benson in, they were making plans about doing something together. Benson had emailed Charon offering to pay his way home, and telling Charon to bring your daughter."

Peterson held up the slip of paper. "Do the Mounties know about this?"

"Not yet. I had a feeling you wanted to be first in line. Want to tell me how come?"

"My daughter," Peterson said.

"I assumed as much. Victim or accomplice?"

Peterson let the question slide.

Gould did not push it.

Peterson said, "I don't want the Mounties coming down on her head."

"Which means you want me to go slow."

Peterson nodded. "But not too slow."

Gould shrugged.

Peterson looked at the address — 2 Bigger Road, Antrim, Nova Scotia.

"I checked out Google Earth on that one," Gould said, chinning toward the slip of paper. "It's past the airport. A lot of woods, and not much else."

• • •

Danny Little was waiting for him in the parking lot. He walked Peterson to his car. Braced both hands against the driver's side door and pressed his head against the roof. Peterson set his back against the rear door. Neither looked at the other, and nothing was said for a long time. Then Danny Little turned to Peterson.

"I didn't want to shoot him," he said. "I was scared to pull the trigger."

"I know," Peterson said. He looked at Danny. "But sometimes . . ."

"I know." Little nodded, then opened the driver's side door, and Peterson got in.

"You need anything?" Little asked.

"No, I'm good. What about you?"

"Time maybe."

"It's never enough," Peterson said.

Little closed the door and walked to where his Malibu was parked.

In his own car, Peterson sat with his arms circling the steering wheel and his head pressed against his hands. When he looked up, he saw Danny watching him. He waved, signalling that he was okay. Little waved back.

• • •

He drove the city streets, taking corners just anywhere. Calibrating his brain by the shrieking street lights and crying shadows. He parked in front of St. Theresa's church, got out, and climbed the crumbly stone steps to sit on the top one. He heard young voices from the junior high across the street, but saw only the school's large shadowy shape beneath several tall maples, which were shedding their leaves.

He thought about Raylene bleeding to death in his arms, and that brought to mind the five-year-old memory of a teenage girl in the Broken Promise country bar. Her name had been Molly Gornish, and she had also bled to death in his arms. He saw their faces pinned like specimens on a wall in a crummy room with a rumpled bed and a window covered with cobwebs. Memories echoed memories.

"Keep yourself human," he mumbled, a mantra he had told others during his twenty-three years as a cop. "Don't roll in the mud with them."

But he had rolled in the mud. Wallowed in it.

As a car passed, its headlights sprayed the shadows across the street. Peterson saw a young couple huddled into a doorway, ducking from the light. Young love, he thought, and flinched at what popped into his head. A second car drove past, and he saw the girl pull away and kick at a pile of leaves that had blown into the doorway. His mind flashed to an eight-year-old boy kicking dead leaves off his mother's grave. Fingering her stone marker. Sobbing.

And he remembered one fall morning more than a year ago, walking with Dr. Heaney along a bridle path in Point Pleasant Park.

"What did your father say?" Dr. Heaney had asked.

Peterson had shrugged off the question at first, then had answered, "He told me not to go there anymore. He said I shouldn't keep thinking about someone who was dead."

Now, Peterson descended the church steps and got into his car. He stopped at a liquor store on his way home. Drove and guzzled, not giving a damn what happened next.

When he turned onto his street, he saw Hillier's silver Lexus parked in his driveway. He pulled in behind it. Hillier got out. Peterson got out, with the bottle of Johnnie Walker in his hand.

"It was on the evening news," Hillier said.

"Nothing to say," Peterson said.

Hillier took the bottle as Peterson fumbled a key into the lock on the front door.

"I'm not looking for company," Peterson said.

They entered the house and turned into the kitchen. Peterson went for the bottle, but Hillier would not give it up.

"You don't need this," Hillier said.

Peterson grit his teeth. "You weren't there."

"What about your daughter?"

"I can't go after her without it."

"Yeah sure," Hillier said. "And then what?"

Peterson stared at him. He wrestled a chair from the table and sat.

Hillier held up the bottle and looked at the label. He turned to the sink and unscrewed the cap. "If you get into this stuff, you won't be going anywhere. And that's something we both know."

Peterson hung his head.

"How come we do things that just make it worse?" Hillier

said, and shook his head sadly. "Punish ourselves over and over, like more hurt will make all the other hurt go away?"

Peterson looked at him.

"You did. I did," Hillier said. "What's wrong with us?"

Peterson did not answer.

Hillier emptied the bottle down the drain.

CHAPTER
FORTY-ONE

Once off Old Guysborough Road, the houses thinned and the woods thickened with maple and birch, losing leaves but still blazing in sunlight. The undergrowth grew dense with a brown-and-rust-coloured tangle of wild shrubs and prickly bushes, which had spread into the storm water ditches along the gravel roads and up onto the shoulders.

Peterson drove. Hillier gave directions according to Google Maps on his iPhone and a *Nova Scotia Atlas* of all highways, roads, houses, buildings, rail lines, and walking trails. Antrim was nothing but a spot on the map. No village or anything like one. No church. No settlement. No cluster of houses.

"Take the next right," Hillier said.

Peterson turned onto Bigger Road, a narrow, deeply rutted dirt road with weeds flourishing in the centre of it.

"If there's one called Smaller Road, you wonder what that

one's like," Hillier said. He shook his head in disgust at a two-storey house collapsed in on itself, raising his voice above the noise of the Chevy rattling over the crusty ridges, in and out of pot holes. "No wonder that Charon grew up whacky."

Peterson did not reply. He had hardly spoken since they had left his house an hour earlier, after they had doubled back so Hillier could get his SIG Sauer from the glove box of the Lexus. Crossing the MacKay Bridge, the morning sun was like a beesting in Peterson's bloodshot eyes. They had followed the 102, exited at the airport, followed Old Guysborough Road for twenty clicks, turned onto a paved secondary road, and then onto Bigger Road.

"Why would anyone live out here?" Hillier continued. "Why come here in the first place?"

Bigger Road took a sweeping left turn, passing large patches of clear-cut. A dozer-scarred woods road branched off to the right and climbed toward high ground and into a hardwood stand, which was still brilliant with colour. Bigger Road continued its leftward sweep and descent toward Ruggs Lake. Runoff ruts grabbed at the Chevy's wheels and pulled the car from one side of the road to the other. Peterson fought to hold the steering wheel straight, riding the ruts and bouncing over potholes and a stretch of mud-hardened ridges.

At a sudden widening of the road, at what looked like a turnaround point, Hillier said in disbelief, "Is this it?"

Peterson stopped the car and looked around, seeing nothing but scrub spruce and spindly birch and popular scattered in a cutover boulder-strewn barren.

Both got out of the car at the same time. Both shrugged at the same time as well.

"Google has been wrong before," Hillier said.

Peterson walked to where a grassed-over path, which was barely wide enough for a vehicle, angled to the left and down toward a boggy area. Twenty metres along the path, they came upon the charred ruins of a house and two small outbuildings.

"This is probably where Charon grew up until his parents died," he said.

They returned to the turnaround point.

"No power poles," Peterson said. "There wasn't one the entire length of this road. These people had been living without electricity. No wonder he went to live with his grandparents."

They got into the car, and Peterson drove to where the woods road branched off and climbed into a hardwood stand. He drove it, and at a clear-cut section stopped. From that height, they had a large view of the countryside surrounding Ruggs Lake and the Charon homestead. Not far in the distance was a gravel road, which dipped south into thick woodland and came within ten kilometres of backing onto the Charon property.

Hillier had the Atlas open on the Chevy's hood and was squinting and tracing his finger along the page. "Bigger Road continues past the Charon house, but isn't much more than an ATV trail. It goes across country and comes out at what looks like a farm on that gravel road." He looked up and pointed at the road in the distance. "I can't make out the name of it on the map."

Peterson rounded the car and had a look at the Atlas. "MacMullin Road," he said, then grunted with a sudden realization. "Charon's password to the dark web is MullMacin."

CHAPTER
FORTY-TWO

They backtracked to where Bigger Road joined the Antrim Road, hung a right, and drove to an area called Dutch Settlement. There they took another right onto McMullin Road. Hillier had the atlas on his lap and was trying to determine where the remains of Bigger Road broke from the woods near a field and a farmhouse.

They passed a dozen or so bungalows and split-levels, all of a style built in the past forty years, and all separated by wide swaths of dense woodland. Most of the houses sat twenty or thirty metres in from the road, but a few had long tree-lined driveways, and some of these were littered with junk cars and pickups. Then the houses thinned to one or two every kilometre or so, then there was a long stretch of nothing but trees and undergrowth. After a few more kilometres of this, Hillier announced they must have gone too far.

Peterson continued driving, looking for a spot where the road widened and he could easily make a three-point turn. At a sharp bend, he suddenly hit the brakes.

"There," he said, and pointed to a white-on-blue sign for the property address — 2170. Power poles ran up a narrow dirt driveway alongside a field of high grass that was scattered with alders and cat spruce. About a hundred metres across the field was an abandoned farmhouse with long poles bracing up one side. Peterson recognized it as the farmhouse in the photo his daughter had emailed him. Large letters had been spray-painted on the side viewed from the road. The letters spelled *Fuck You*.

He crept the car along the shoulder and tucked it tight to a drainage ditch and behind a growth of saplings and bushes.

"Sit tight," he ordered.

"No way," Hillier said. "You go, I go."

Peterson reached for the nail puller under the driver's seat, and Hillier snapped a fifteen-round clip into the SIG Sauer.

"Keep that in your belt," Peterson said. "I don't want it going off by accident."

"I know how to use it," Hillier griped.

They got out, eased the car doors closed, and ducked low, hugging the edge of the ditch as they made their way to where the field ended and thick forest began. Keeping just inside the tree line, they headed into the woods and negotiated their way toward the farmhouse. Peterson in the lead, holding branches so they did not whip back into Hillier's face.

They stopped abreast of the farmhouse, which stood in the centre of the field less than fifty metres from where they were standing. The blue Ford Explorer that had trailed Peterson was parked in back. Not far beyond that was a dilapidated hay barn with one door missing and the other hanging by its hinges. Beside the barn, an outhouse had been blown over. The forest had started reclaiming a fallow back field.

Hillier was about to say something when the back door slammed open and Charon stepped out and down the rickety porch. Charon held a short length of rope, and on the other end, with the rope around her neck, was Britney Comer. Her hands were tied behind her back. Peterson recognized her at once. Her face now drained of a young woman's vitality. Her walk sluggish, shoulders stooped.

They watched as Charon led her across the yard to the barn, forced her inside, untied her hands, and ordered her to do what she had to do. From their angle, Peterson and Hillier could see her pull down her jeans and panties, and squat. They heard Charon's menacing voice, but could not make out what he was saying to her. When she was done, he retied her hands and pulled her back across the yard and into the house.

From inside the house, Peterson heard his daughter say something in a loud voice, and then Charon yelled that if she didn't do what she was told, he would fuck her up with nothing to pop or shoot. Then Peterson heard smashing sounds and the shatter of glass. A woman screamed, but Peterson could not determine if it was Katy or Britney screaming. He dropped the nail puller from up his sleeve and into his hand and was about to sprint to the back door when Hillier reached for his arm and told him to take it easy.

"Rush it and we risk losing the element of surprise," he said.

Peterson nodded and replaced the nail puller up his sleeve. "As soon as it gets dark, I'm going in," he said.

"Not alone," Hillier countered, giving Peterson a forceful look.

"Alone," Peterson insisted. "I need you here in case things don't go the way I want them to."

"Sitting on my hands, or what?"

Peterson pointed at the SIG Sauer in Hillier's belt. "You said you know how to use that thing."

For the next few hours, they sat silently side by side on the trunk of a fallen tree and waited for darkness. Both listened for sounds coming from inside the house. Hillier fidgeted. Nervous. Peterson was no less anxious.

All the while, Charon's voice was constant. Most of what he said was too low for Peterson and Hillier to understand. But sometimes he became agitated, and when he did, his voice rose and his words became clearer. Once he raved about one of the cameras not working as well as he wanted it to.

"I want everyone to see it," he had shouted. "And that goddamn camera up where she is . . . The fucking thing keeps cutting out."

Peterson took the "up where she is" to mean an upstairs bedroom. He took little comfort in knowing where Charon had locked up Britney Comer because it meant he would have to climb to the second floor to get her out.

A half hour later they heard Charon throwing things from the sound of it, and screaming at the top of his lungs about Benson not showing up. And that clicked with what Jamie Gould had said about Benson and Charon making plans to do something together.

After a while of relative quiet, Charon yelled at Katy. He called her a fucking whore, a dopehead, and a goddamn useless bitch.

"You too," he had shouted. "Stop crying. You do what I said to do or I light you up too."

Peterson's face drained. His fists clenched. Hillier reached for Peterson's arm to hold him back.

An hour later the sun set, and soon after that the moon rose as a thin crescent. Although the stars appeared so much brighter this far from the city, the farmyard and backfield were still as dark as a confessional. The scatter of young fir trees and scrub bushes were black clumps, conveniently spaced for someone ducking from one to another.

Incandescent light escaped the spaces between the boards covering the windows and drew yellow slivers on the house-shadowed ground.

Hillier whispered, "How much longer?"

Peterson whispered, "Give it another hour."

They went back to sitting and listening to activity inside the house. Someone clomping on a set of stairs. A woman crying. A loud groan. Then Charon shouting, "Yeah, there it is."

Then there was a long stretch of quiet, and then Peterson stood to go.

Hillier leaned over with his whole body, as though stricken with stomach cramps.

"I'm scared," he whispered.

"I'd be worried if you weren't," Peterson consoled. "Give me half an hour to get up and inside the house. Then wait ten minutes. If I don't call out, you come in."

"Are you sure you don't want the gun?" Hillier encouraged.

Peterson shook his head.

He slowly worked his way along the tree line to a position that was twenty metres on the far side of the barn. There was a dense thicket to the left of the barn. Peterson lowered to the ground and crawled from among the trees toward the thicket. It took him a few minutes to crawl that far. From that angle, Peterson had a clear view of the back porch and through the open door into the kitchen, which was lighted by a bare bulb hanging from the ceiling.

Next to a brick chimney there was a pine hutch with empty shelves, and beside that an old black cookstove. A long harvest table stood in the centre of the room. A laptop computer was on top of it.

Just then Katy walked into the kitchen and sat at the table. Her brown hair hung past her shoulders, and she was so skinny that she looked frail.

Peterson's eyes filled as he watched her tap a key on the desktop and wake it from sleep. She turned her head to the open door as though looking for someone, then played the mouse pad and deliberately, as though forcing her index fingers to do what her brain wanted them to do, struck several keys on the keyboard. Again she played the mouse pad, leaning into the effort, struggling to move the cursor where she wanted it.

She got up from the chair, then quickly sat back down. Again she played the mouse pad and clicked. The computer screen cut to black. She got up and stepped toward the open door.

As he quickly jumped to his feet to make a break for the house, his cell phone vibrated in his pocket. At the same time, he heard something move from the thicket. He turned toward the sound, and a sudden blow caught him on the left shoulder. It buckled his knees. Stunned. He dropped the nail puller into his hand. Rose on his toes and pivoted to his left. There was another sudden movement from the thicket. The next blow struck the back of his neck. He fell face first into the high grass, and his brain hollowed into an unfeeling blackness.

CHAPTER
FORTY-THREE

Voices inside his head. Images. Memories. A stream dark with overhanging branches. A boy hanging from one of them. Crying. Letting go and falling. Falling.

"Are you still dreaming about falling?"

Plunging into the dark pool and not touching bottom. Gasping for air and reaching to his mother in a third-floor window and seeing her turn away.

"Do you dream it often?"

Working his hands into fists. Punching walls. One-on-one with himself in a corner of a room with the lights out. A loaded .38 in his right hand. Safety on. Safety off. Staring it down. Staring at his wife's drunken face screaming at him. His own drunken face screaming back.

Streets and alleys. Hard-mouthed faces in the shadows watching him crying at his wife's grave. Looking away from the grave, then looking down and seeing the teen lying on the barroom floor with her wrist slashed. Bleeding into his arms.

"I still don't sleep. I still can't turn on the lights in that house. Afraid."

"What are you afraid of?"

"That sound."

"What sound?"

"A round being chambered."

He felt as though he was hanging by his wrists, and that a hammer was pounding in his head. The voices continued.

"I couldn't trust what I was feeling."

"And what was that?"

"Scared. I was so scared."

He opened his eyes and saw he was in a room where sunlight seeped through cracks between the boards over a window, and lit by a bare bulb in a ceiling fixture in a hallway. He could see down the hallway and through a half-open door. He closed his eyes and flinched at the pounding in his head. The voices continued.

"Drinking more. Hurting people. Losing track. Are you writing this down?"

"I'm also recording it."

"Recording?"

"So you can hear what we talked about."

He suddenly realized he was sitting naked with his back against a wall and that there were leather straps on his wrists. They were tied to bolts in the wall and held his arms above his head. The voices came from across the room: a recording of his private sessions with Dr. Heaney.

He pressed his hands against the wall and, using the straps for support, tried lifting his body enough to set his legs to stand. But the angle into which his arms twisted flashed pain across his shoulders and down his arms. He sank back to the floor.

All the while the recorded voices continued.

"I can't get back the years," he heard himself saying.

And Dr. Heaney replied, "Of course not, but you can make up for them."

"I don't know how."

"You mean you haven't tried."

"How can I try?"

Peterson heard someone coming. The door opened wider. He ducked his head from the increased light then lifted it.

Against the bright incandescent light stood a silhouette. The recorded voices stopped playing. Then the silhouette spoke, and by the sound of the voice, Peterson knew it was David Charon.

"We get so little time," Charon said. "To waste what we get, to fritter it away, to hate yourself for all those lost moments. I mean how much time and energy have you wasted. I listened to everything you told that psychiatrist. We both did. Crying over spilt milk." His voice changed to a falsetto. "Oh Mommy, Mommy, help me. I've lost my way."

Charon laughed then said, "And now you've found it, and it led you here, to me."

He switched on the overhead light in the room, and the sudden brightness stabbed at Peterson's eyes. Charon pointed to a camera mounted above the door. "And the whole world will be watching."

Peterson blinked away the hard light and speed-scanned the room. Broken plaster on the ceiling and walls. Exposed wooden slats and studs. Wooden floorboards. No base-board, and no door and window frames. On the floor, just inside the door, was a small black wireless speaker, and beside the speaker was an unlighted eight-inch red column candle. There was a boarded window on the wall to his right. In the centre of the room stood a single ladder-back wooden chair. Otherwise the room was empty.

He studied the leather straps fastened to his wrist, and saw how they were similarly tied to what he calculated to be three-inch eyebolts with no more than an inch and a half screwed into the wall studs.

Charon stepped farther into the room, sure of himself, flicking his long hair away from his face. Grinning. But not his eyes. They were fixed in a wicked stare. He sat in the chair. For a long time he continued to stare at Peterson. He again pointed to the camera above the door.

"Can you imagine if there were cameras in Hell," he said, his voice almost dreamy. "An upload to the Internet. Website where people can watch the suffering. There'd be a line six times around the world with people changing their tune. Down on their knees, begging for salvation."

He got up and knelt beside Peterson. Face to face.

"Or maybe the world would watch it and love it, like with a porno film. Get it up, you know, feel the urge to hurt, break bones. Kill." He smiled contemptuously. "Herd them into a house and tie them up." From a hip pocket he pulled out a pack of matches. He lit one and held it up and stared into the flame.

"It wouldn't be Hell no more," he crooned happily. "Not if everyone wanted to go."

He extended his arm so the match was an inch from

Peterson's cheek. Peterson tried not to flinch, but when the heat became too intense, he blew it out.

Charon laughed. He checked the straps on Peterson's wrists. Tugged on them to ensure the bolts were still tight in the studs.

Peterson's daughter entered the room with a wobbly, vacant expression. He quickly raised one knee and tried to turn his hips to hide his sex, ashamed to have his daughter see him naked.

Charon followed Peterson's eyes to the doorway.

"Get over here," he ordered.

Katy did not move.

"I said get over here."

She still did not move.

Charon stomped to the doorway and grabbed her by the hair and dragged her to stand in front of her father.

"Tell him what you told me," Charon said.

Katy squirmed against the grip Charon had on her hair.

"Tell him!"

"What?" she muttered.

"That you hate him," Charon said.

"I hate you," she mumbled.

"Say it again," Charon commanded.

Katy looked down at Peterson. She clutched her shoulders as though holding herself together. In a dispirited voice she said, "I hate you."

Peterson saw her bruised face, the awkward angle of her jaw, slit for a smile, sad eyes. Like so many he had known working the streets, being trafficked by pimps, wasting away with whatever they can get in their arms or up their noses, he saw a young woman racked with the desperate need for something that would quiet her hands and make her world go away.

Charon must have sensed the insincerity in her words because he abruptly turned on her and, with a closed fist, punched her in the chest.

She went sprawling toward the door, caught her breath, and began crawling from the room. Crying.

Peterson struggled to get free, the leather straps tightening on his wrists. He shouted at Charon, calling him a goddamn coward.

Charon spun toward the kneeling, defenceless Peterson and swiftly kicked him in the stomach. Then Charon's face split into a senseless grin. He pointed to the ceiling-mounted camera.

"Thermal," he said. "It sees through smoke." He turned back to Peterson and crouched down to go eye-to-eye with him. His voice became low but menacing. "Right now, right here, how about I fuck your daughter. What do you say?"

Peterson stared at him.

Over his shoulder Charon called to Katy. "Come back here."

"No," Peterson begged and struggled against the bonds. But his struggle only further tightened the straps. "No." His voice cracked. He saw Katy get to her feet and hobble from the room.

Charon faced the camera and stuck out his tongue. "Whatever I do, it's me doing it," he said. He turned to Peterson. "What's left after that? Nothing. Not a fucking thing." He started to laugh. Stopped. Then suddenly left the room.

A minute or so later, he returned and stood over Peterson.

"Just so you know," he said, and held out Hillier's pistol. "You got nothing to hope for." He laughed, and when he stopped laughing, he said, "You and the one upstairs, this is your Hell. You just burn and burn, until the fire burns you up. Five-star. Now that's sweet."

CHAPTER
FORTY-FOUR

Hours passed. Daylight no longer seeped between the boards covering the window. Periodically Peterson shifted his legs from side to side to keep them from falling asleep. No food. No water. No place to relieve himself. With the light in the hallway turned off, the room was dark. But dark would not hide him from the thermal camera. Still he tried to get free by looping one of the straps over the ring of the bolt, hoping it would catch firmly enough that he could pull down to unscrew it from the wall stud. Each time the strap slipped on the smooth metal. He tried that a dozen times then gave up.

He then used his legs to lift his body enough to slacken the tension on the leather straps. He grabbed the round eye of the bolt with his right hand and strained to turn it counter-clockwise. The bolt did not budge. He continued until his arm ached. He switched arms and tried to turn the other bolt several times. It did not budge either. He sank back on the floor to give his arm muscles a rest.

From down the hall he heard Charon's muffled voice, along with the faint clicking sounds of a keyboard. He guessed that the room at the end of the hallway was the kitchen. Charon yelled something about Benson. Then something smashed as though it had been thrown against a wall or on the floor.

The recording of Peterson and Heaney's private sessions started playing.

"I just don't want to talk about it," Peterson was saying on the recording.

"Then why are we here?" Dr. Heaney asked.

"I know, but it's not what I want to talk about, not now."

"Why not now?"

On the recording, Peterson did not answer.

"You said once before that you had to do it," Dr. Heaney urged.

"That doesn't make it right," Peterson said.

"No it doesn't. And that's one of the most difficult things to reconcile, doing what we believe we have to do, yet knowing it is wrong." There was a long pause, then Heaney asked, "So what happened?"

"I had a shotgun."

For the next few minutes, he sat naked in that dark room in the farmhouse and listened to himself crying on the recording, begging someone, anyone, for something he could not put into words.

The recording stopped. Charon stepped from the kitchen and switched on the hall light. He walked into the room in which Peterson was being held, turned on the ceiling light, and sat on the chair. He stared at Peterson and did not speak for a long time.

Peterson could see Charon was stoned.

"Used-up cop. Last hurrah," Charon finally said.

Peterson did not respond.

"A waste," Charon continued. "Miserable husband. Lousy father. A fucking crybaby. Over what? Huh? What were you crying about?"

Peterson still would not give Charon the benefit of a response.

"You blow people apart then bawl your eyes out," Charon continued. "You got no sack. You got no idea what makes it go around. What that shrink was talking about, right and wrong? Where does that come from? Like who makes the rules? Ten Commandments? Thou shalt not do this and that? Nothing but bullshit. Nothing but God riding the top rung telling us to back off from doing what gets us off, like He wasn't up there showing us how. Lightning bolts and shit. Egging the Jews to slaughter thousands. The man going five-star and watching it like it was an upload site in heaven. Blueprint for what I'm doing. No different. Only I'm not rolling up big sleeves and making people out of mud, calling them good or beautiful, then wasting their asses. Women and children. Hoarding it all for Himself. Telling us Thou shalt not kill. And you know how come? Because it's the gore and killing that makes us like Him. That's the real story. Men like gods. Adam eating that fucking apple then going down on Eve. Opening his eyes to what really turns him on. Thumbing his nose and feeling the urge to crush it all. Upload it, fucking right, five-star, and letting God see what He started."

Charon faced the ceiling-mounted camera and held out his hands, palms up. His face went rapturous, and his voice sounded almost ethereal.

"Holding life," he said. He extended his arms and brought his hands together. "Holding it like it was something precious, something so fucking beautiful." He suddenly snapped his fingers closed and sneered. "Then watching it die. Just like that."

Peterson kept a straight face through it all. Then he said, "Like what you did to Stephanie Zola."

Charon turned to him. "I got bored," he said and flashed a shit-eating grin. "My grandfather showed me how. Hanging cows and pigs in the barn to bleed them out. Going at the carcass with a cleaver."

He turned away, switched off the light, and left the room.

Sometime later, Peterson heard a car fire up and drive off. Not long after that, his daughter entered the room and, without looking at him or saying a word to him, slipped a broken piece of glass into his right hand. He grasped it, careful not to let it cut.

"Katy," he appealed as she turned away and walked from the room. "The mistakes I made," he called after her. "I'm sorry."

He heard the back door open and close, and her steps down the back porch. He listened intently to determine which way she had gone, but heard nothing but an upstairs floorboard yawn, followed by someone's restless stirring.

"Britney," he called.

No answer.

He called a second time. No answer.

He listened for the car returning. Not hearing it, he carefully worked the piece of glass from his palm to between his thumb and index finger. With his legs positioned to lift his body to slacken the leather straps, he began sliding the glass back and forth across the strap. The strokes were short, and the sharp edge prevented him from pressing it against his palm and applying pressure. After a dozen or so strokes, he felt the cut line with his middle finger. The glass had hardly scored the leather.

He continued, pausing now and again to test the cut line, as well as listen for the car's return. Mostly he heard the faint breathings of an old wooden house.

The work went slow. Too slow. He cut faster. The strap suddenly shifted against the metal bolt. The glass slipped and he barely caught it between his little finger and the heel of his hand.

He was a long time working the glass back up his palm; one finger holding it while a lower one painstakingly manoeuvred it upward in tiny increments. At last, he had the glass between his thumb and index finger and started cutting. A slow, steady rhythm. Eyes straining. Teeth clenched. His middle finger tested for progress, and he figured he was a quarter of the way through the strap. He was so focused that he did not hear the car engine until it neared the house.

The car door opened. Peterson heard Katy scream. The car door slammed shut.

Then he heard Charon drag her into the house, through the kitchen, and along the hall. The whole time she was screaming and begging, swearing to him that she had not been running away. Peterson heard cloth being torn, then the sound of her body pounding against the stair treads as Charon dragged her to the second floor. Then there was the distinct sound of a fist striking flesh. Her screaming stopped. Charon said to her, "I read the text you sent him."

Peterson cut the leather like mad. He gripped the glass and pressed down. It cut into his thumb and finger, and into his palm. Blood dripped to the floor. He kept working the glass, and it cut deeper into the leather and into his flesh.

Then he heard Charon descend the stairs. His head shot up. His thumb slipped, and the glass dropped to the floor.

"Damn!" he shouted. He cringed at the tightening in his stomach. His legs lost strength, and his body slumped.

"Katy," he groaned. "Katy."

Charon passed along the hall and through the kitchen. He made a couple of trips to the car. He entered Peterson's room, switched on the overhead, kicked aside the chair, and set a large plastic jar and a can on the floor.

"You're the one without sack," Peterson provoked, at the same time reading the contents of the jar and can. "Punching women. No guts. You're a goddamn coward. A failure."

The jar contained crystallized chlorine. The can held brake fluid.

Charon turned to him with a cruel smile. "Benson in jail, his brother dead." He looked around the room then back at Peterson. "Roast pork, you hear what I'm saying." He went back outside.

Peterson set his legs to get all the strength he could from his thighs. He yanked at the cut strap. Once. Twice. On the third try, it snapped off the ringbolt.

He then reached his free hand to untie the other one, but the knot was so tight he could not undo it. He looked for the piece of glass on the floor. It had landed more than a metre away. He stretched his right leg and extended his toes, but the glass was just out of reach. He shifted his body and tried again. No dice.

The backdoor opened and slammed shut.

Peterson quickly returned to his sitting position with his arms above his head, making it appear as though both wrists were still tied to the bolts.

Charon entered, carrying an armload of kindling. He dropped it beside the jar and can.

"I watched your videos," Peterson said, still trying to provoke. "Five-star my ass."

Charon ignored him. He emptied the jar of crystallized chlorine onto the floor then tented the kindling over it. He pulled the tab on the can of brake fluid.

"Tough guy who couldn't go at someone straight on," Peterson continued. "Women and girls. That's your style. Chicken shit. You and Benson."

Charon looked at him. "He wanted a part in this," he snickered. "Now he won't even get to watch." He poured the brake fluid over the chlorine. He stood. "Five minutes, maybe." He pointed at the camera. "Say cheese." He backed out of the room and ran from the house.

Peterson heard the car start and drive off. He pried his fingernails at the knot. Getting nowhere. Digging harder.

The mixture in the centre of the room suddenly started to bubble and smoulder. His eyes widened. His body tensed. Frantic, he grabbed the ringbolt with both hands and howled at the effort to turn it. It did not budge.

The mixture burst into a torch flaming high to the ceiling. The kindling caught fire, and within seconds the fire spread to the floor. At first, white smoke rose from the flaming mixture, but as the fire spread to the dried wooden floor, walls, and ceiling, the smoke turned a dark grey.

Peterson tried again to turn the bolt. Crouching. Groaning for strength. Shouting down the pain in his knuckles. He felt it give. In the same instant, his head snapped back from the sharp, burning smell of bleach.

"Oh Christ," he shouted. He gripped the bolt and came onto it with everything he had. It turned, and kept turning.

By now flames engulfed the downstairs and were burning through to the second floor. Dry timbers, floor planks, and lath walls burned like tinder. The entire front of the hundred-year-old farmhouse screamed with the blaze that was burning so hot iron nails exploded like gunshots.

He found the piece of glass on the floor and bolted into the hall. His terrified face was red from the heat. At the foot of the stairs, he stepped into a pile of clothes on the floor, realizing now that Charon must have stripped Katy before dragging her upstairs. He reached down, found a torn shirt, ripped it in half, and tied half over his nose and mouth.

Britney and Katy were wildly screaming. He climbed through thick smoke and intense heat. Felt his way along the upstairs hall to a room that was directly above the one he had been held in. It was filled with smoke. Fire burned up the outside wall, fed by a steady wind, and licked into the room from between the cracks in the clapboard.

He found Katy and tied the other half of the shirt over her nose and mouth, all the while talking through her panic. He ran the piece of glass over the leather straps that held her. First one pulled apart then the other. He stooped, swung her over his shoulder, and ran for the stairs. Falling down them as much as running. Through the kitchen and out of the burning building. He ran ten, twenty, thirty metres into the field before setting her safely on the ground.

His breath came in gasps, and in the pupils of his eyes were individual tongues of fire. When he heard Comer screaming from inside the fiery house, fear overwhelmed him. His whole body betrayed the terror he felt. He started to cry and shook his fists.

Comer screamed again, and continued screaming. He gathered his nerve and patted the ground for the piece of glass he had dropped. After finding it, he then removed the torn shirt from Katy's conscious, stricken face. He started back into the house. From the narrow hall, the fire whirled through the kitchen and straight at him. He ducked back onto the porch and fell to the ground, hugging it and shaking all over. He drew a deep breath, retied the torn shirt over his mouth and nose, and crawled back to the porch. He re-entered the house and kept low to escape the smoke and flames, and to suck the air that the fire was drawing along the floor through the open door. He straightened to look for the stairs. He could not see them. He dropped back down and crawled further. He crawled into a wall. Felt left and right. A dead end. He swung around and crawled back.

Flames were up the walls and flaring across the ceiling. The heat was so intense it burned his bare skin. He stood and looked for the stairs. He could not see them. He dropped back down and extended his arms to feel walls on either side. He walked forward on his knees until his right hand felt the opening. On hands and knees he climbed the burning stairs through the choking smoke and under an archway of flames.

At the head of the stairs, he turned left, following Comer's screams. A closed door was hot to his touch. He stood, gritted his teeth, shut his eyes, and shouldered open the door into a blast of smoke that stuffed his lungs. For an instant he held fire in his arms then tossed it aside. He dropped to the floor. Beneath the smoke and flames, he saw Comer tied to ring bolts in a corner of the room. She, too, was naked. Her face stretched into a look of sheer terror. Yellow paint bubbled off the walls around her.

He crawled the fire-licked floorboards. When he reached her, the bubbling paint burst into flames. He frantically cut through the leather ties on her wrists then reached for her hand, but she was too frightened to respond. He tried to say something, but the smoke and flames were so intense he could not find his voice. He tried tying the torn shirt over her face and had to overcome her confused effort to fight him off. He gathered her into his arms, shielded her with his big body, and carried her to the stairs. He stumbled and skidded off the treads, then broadened his shoulders to steady himself between the fiery walls of the stairway. Fire burned his shoulders, his chest, and up his back and over his neck. His hair was on fire. His face contorted and he howled from the burning and loosened his grip. She slipped from his arms and disappeared beneath the billowing smoke. He cried out at losing her. The intense pain sucked his strength. He stooped and groped through the smoke. Felt her arm and pulled her into his arms to shield her from the flames. Down the hall he staggered, through the open door, and over the flame-engulfed porch. He carried her across the field, dropped her beside his daughter, and fell to the ground a burned mass of pain.

Flames roared through the roof. The house seemed to shake with the heat then buckle. Then came a loud groan from the burning building, and the roof collapsed.

CHAPTER
FORTY-FIVE

IV drips of morphine and fentanyl. A bodysuit and helmet of bandages. Excruciating pain when they changed his position on the bed, sending high voltage through his entire body. Sometimes he heard voices in the room. Sometimes he had a sense of someone quietly standing or sitting beside him. Sometimes a kaleidoscope of images flashed through the pain. And sometimes thoughts and memories tangled as they unfolded in his mind.

Whoosh.

"Good morning, Mr. Peterson," a voice said. "My name is Susan. I'll be your nurse again today."

He sensed her moving from his feet to his side. Her voice was clear and distinct.

"You have been in hospital two days, Intensive Care. You have severe burns. There are bandages on your eyes and on most of your body."

What she said was what other nurses had said. Keeping him informed. Up to date. Removing layers of anxiety. Or trying to.

"The noise you hear is a ventilator," she continued. "It's breathing for you through a tube in your throat. Your lungs suffered damage in the fire."

Whoosh.

Breath of life. A machine playing God. The dry taste of honey from the rock. And then the pain struck at him. It gnawed and gnawed, swirling his mind with images of a corn maze in a farmer's field and a confusion of stairways and corridors with numbered doors. Dead ends and wrong turns. A switchback down to a garden bench where a woman's body dangled from a tree branch. A Skype call. A woman's voice begging him. "Please, Daddy. Please."

Whoosh.

"I'm sorry, Mr. Peterson, but we will have to move you again."

His cry of protest choked on the tube in his throat.

"I'll increase your pain medication before we do. We'll give it time to take effect."

Beneath a fold of coloured cloth in his mind, he heard a woman's voice, not nearby, but near enough. "I don't know what that means."

And he heard someone explain. "It means he has third degree burns on fifty percent of his body."

A drugged slurry of thoughts and feelings. Lights and shadows. And when a shadow moved, fear pulsed in his blood.

"As gentle as we can. On three."

The pain exploded into a fiery wheel of faces. Young women's faces. Dead faces. Angry faces. His wife's face. His daughter's. Shouting at him from a closed window in a red brick building, and from the top and bottom of a burning stairway.

The truth of it. The why. A jigsaw puzzle. Pieces that don't fit. Words. Feelings. Sounds. A muddy voice saying, "Woe to you within the grip of the burning." And from far away his cell phone ringing. Ringing.

"What about his eyes?"

"The doctors haven't determined the severity of the damage."

Dreams and nightmares. Seeps of unwanted memories. And moments of clarity sneaking out from behind the pain-killers and the pain.

Bernie's voice whispered from somewhere far away. "I had to see for myself."

"And?" Danny's voice whispered back.

"Charred building. And there were two guys standing in the middle of it. One walks over. A tired looking guy in a red jump suit."

"Lonny Day," Danny said. "Fire inspector."

Peterson fought through the drugs to listen to their distant voices, which seemed woven into the pattern of hospital sounds.

"The other guy was in jeans. Red shirt, blue insignia. I thought they were scavengers at first. They told me they already knew where the fire had started, and how. The fire inspector . . ."

"Lonny Day."

"He said a neighbour saw the flames shooting above the trees. He called it in. Volunteer fire department was already geared up for a training exercise. They were there in less than ten minutes. An ambulance in twelve."

"Lucky," Danny said.

"Especially for Comer and his daughter. They were lucky he was there to get them out."

The tube strangled the words he wanted to say. The pain shackled his body from moving. He recognized Susan's voice.

"You can go closer and talk to him," she said. "He can hear."

"Really?" Danny said.

"We weren't sure," Bernie said.

"I know what it says about visitor restrictions," the nurse said, "but so long as you're masked and gowned. He can't talk yet, but we worked out a system with his finger. Up and down is 'yes,' back and forth is 'no.'"

He sensed someone step to the side of the bed and crouch down.

"It's Bernie."

He moved his finger up and down.

"Danny's here too. We came to see how you're doing. I mean . . . You know what I mean."

He moved his finger up and down.

"Your daughter and Comer are doing good," she said. "Katy visited the first few days. But . . . She's in rehab working it through. Her choice. She wants to shake it. I think she will. Have faith."

He moved his finger up and down.

"Your friend Cotter wants to come, but they have restrictions. Danny and I badged our way in."

Now Danny's voice came close. "You went overboard this time, Peterson. Attention getter."

There was a self-conscious pause, then Danny continued. "Just so you know, Bernie's not going out on a limb by herself. Me and Richie Leighton will be with her. Yeah, I know, sometimes it just comes down to that."

Peterson heard Danny step back from the bed. Then he heard him step forward. His voice was now real close to Peterson's ear.

"You did good, Peterson," he whispered. "You did pretty goddamn good."

CHAPTER
FORTY-SIX

Sleep was a blessing, whether drug induced or not. It was also a curse when he woke filled with anxiety.

"Good evening, Mr. Peterson."

Not knowing, but sensing.

"I'll be taking vitals and then changing your IV bag."

Hall traffic. Voices.

Hours. Days.

"It is Dr. Demos, Mr. Peterson. We're going to remove the bandage on your eyes and gradually introduce light."

Voices became blurs. Blurs became people. Dr. Demos with six hairs to make a beard. Nurse Susan the girl next door. And another nurse, Alison from St. John's, Newfoundland, heavyset with gentle hands and an accent he liked to listen to.

Skin grafts. The painful unclogging of the tube in his

throat. Choking. Sleeping. Dreaming. His dark world some-times a nightmare.

At last they removed the tube from his throat.

"On a scale of one to ten, with ten being severe, how would you describe the pain when you speak?" Dr. Demos requested.

A long silence. A swallow.

"I don't," Peterson croaked. "I . . . five."

More skin grafts. Physiotherapy.

Then Cotter showed up and smiled to see Peterson sit-ting up in bed. He passed up the hard wooden chair and took the blue padded one.

"Patty's not coming, is she?" Peterson asked. Tight eyes, like he was looking for something he had to squint to see.

Cotter frowned.

"Too much to ask, right?" Peterson said.

"She tried," Cotter explained. "She came by The Office the other night and told me about it, what she felt. Patty's a good woman, but at this stage in the game, for her, she can't deal with this. Anyway, she said you both knew it was over before this happened."

Peterson shrugged. Nodded.

"Let's face it," Cotter continued. "The only reason you and me get along is because . . . I don't know why we get along. Maybe because we're both hard to get along with. I think we both have trouble getting along with ourselves."

Peterson shrugged. "You got a way, you know that."

"Yeah, I know. Silver-tongued devil. What else do you want to know about?"

Peterson caught a breath.

Cotter cackled a laugh. "Katy asked me not to tell. She wanted it to be a surprise."

"A surprise?"

"Yeah. She got a day pass. A few more weeks, and then she'll be living with Bernie until you come home. Yeah, I know, like living with a cop again is therapy. But she can hack it. She's tough, like her old man. And she's doing just fine."

Peterson smiled happily.

Cotter folded his arms and proudly canted his head.

"She's in the lounge waiting her turn," Cotter added.

That had them both laughing. Then Cotter forced them both to change gears. "Bad news."

Peterson looked at him with anxious eyes.

"One of the neighbours out there found Hillier's body covered in leaves."

Peterson went inside himself for a few minutes and then came out.

Cotter waited a moment longer then said, "They caught David Charon."

Peterson closed his eyes.

"He was sitting in a Vancouver coffee shop," Cotter continued. "When they searched his flat on Pandora Street, they found the SIG Sauer registered to Jonathan Hillier. One round fired."

Cotter got up and eased his way to the door. "Yeah, and by the way, that thing we talked about, The Office, being partners? My offer still stands."

"You're not afraid I'll scare away customers?"

"No more than you already do."

Cotter left, and a couple of minutes later Katy entered. She had combed her hair back into a stylish do. Creamy complexion. Red-and-white checked shirt over black slacks. She threw him a hip-high wave. "Hi, Dad."

From under the bedsheet he brought out a burn-scarred hand and waved back.

She sat in the padded chair.

He stared at her and saw her eyes fill. His did the same. He started to say something, but she shook him off. She gently reached for his hand. He smiled and started to cry. She did too.

At ECW Press, we want you to enjoy this book in whatever format you like, whenever you like. Leave your print book at home and take the eBook to go! Purchase the print edition and receive the eBook free. Just send an email to ebook@ecwpress.com and include:

Get the
eBook free!*

*proof of purchase
required

- the book title
- the name of the store where you purchased it
- your receipt number
- your preference of file type: PDF or ePub

A real person will respond to your email with your eBook attached. And thanks for supporting an independently owned Canadian publisher with your purchase!